# Liara Tamani

# Calling My Name

Greenwillow Books

*An Imprint of HarperCollinsPublishers*

Calling My Name

Copyright © 2017 by Liara Tamani

First published in hardcover by Greenwillow Books in 2017; first paperback publication, 2018.

The excerpts from Rita Dove's poems "Gospel" and "Roast Possum" on pages 221, 222, and 223 are from *Thomas and Beulah*, Carnegie-Mellon University Press, © 1986 by Rita Dove. Reprinted by permission of the author. All rights reserved.

The text of this book is set in Perpetua. Book design by Sylvie Le Floc'h.

Library of Congress Cataloging-in-Publication Data
Names: Tamani, Liara, author.
Title: Calling my name / by Liara Tamani.
Description: First edition. | New York : Greenwillow Books, an imprint of HarperCollinsPublishers, [2017] | Summary: "Taja Brown, growing up in a conservative and tightly knit African American family, battles family expectations to discover a sense of self and find her unique voice and purpose"—Provided by publisher.
Identifiers: LCCN 2017029705 | ISBN 9780062656865 (hardback) | ISBN 9780062656872 (pbk. ed.)
Subjects: | CYAC: Coming of age—Fiction. | Family life—Texas—Fiction. | African Americans—Fiction. | Texas—Fiction.
Classification: LCC PZ7.1.T355 Cal 2017 | DDC [Fic]—dc23 LC record available at https://lccn.loc.gov/2017029705

20 21 22 PC/LSCC 10 9 8 7 6 5 4 3

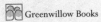 Greenwillow Books

*For my family, who fill me with so much love*

# Contents

A MOVEMENT 1

KICKBALL ON CHRISTMAS EVE 10

BREATHING ROOM 17

HUNGRY SUNDAY 19

THE SWEETEST THING 30

FREESTYLE 41

SOLO 55

IN THE MIDDLE 66

TURQUOISE SKY 78

BLACK-INFESTED 83

GOLD HOOPS 85

A DIRTY SECRET 89

DEEP DIMPLES 95

CHOCOLATE MOURNING 103

ABOUT TIME 106

WAVES 109

GOD DON'T LIKE UGLY 116

ON YOUR MARKS 121

THE GOOD NEWS 128

MR. FRANKLIN 137

LOST IT 147

A DIRTY JOB 153

SHINY HARD BOTTOMS 157

LETTERS 160

EXALTED BEGINNINGS 164

WALLS CAN WAIT 167

IMMUNITY BOOST 173

CUPS OF TEA 176

THAT GIRL 179

THE HARD TRUTH 183

GOOD GUIDES 188


PICKLES AND PUNCH 203

NOTHING TO BE AFRAID OF 206

A BEATING 211

S FOR . . . 216

A DEEP CONVERSATION 220

CHANGE DUE 224

GHOST STAINS 226


SHARP 235

OFF MY CHEST 242

I CAN'T 246

DELIVERY 248

TRYING TO TELL YOU SOMETHING 250

REVELATIONS 254

THE PRICE OF ADMISSION 257

ALMOST EVERYTHING 261

LIFE AFTER DEATH 266


THE DEEP BLUE 271

SO MUCH PROMISE 278

DOUBLE DATE 285

SWEET-BITTER ROUNDS 288

FORGET THAT 294

CALLING MY NAME 303

*She was sure of it, now that she was awake.*

*For she was awake. This was awakeness.*

—Gwendolyn Brooks, *Maud Martha*

# A Movement

There's something moving inside the walls of my body. It's tiptoeing across the high arches of my feet, break-dancing on my kneecaps, running figure eights around my hips as if they're orange cones at recess, skipping up my sides, and climbing up to my shoulders' peaks before swinging across my chest, back and forth, to a steady beat.

Gospel music plays inside the pink wall beside my bed but I don't sing along. The smell of bacon flows from the kitchen, but I don't get up to steal a piece from the pile I know is stacked high on a plate atop grease-soaked napkins. Naima, getting ready in the bed under me, keeps chanting,

"Taja's gonna get in trouble, Taja's gonna get in trouble," but I don't open my mouth to tell her, "Shut up." Nor do I open my eyes. I don't move. I'm busy noticing I'm alive.

For the first time I'm aware that I'm the only one living inside my body, the only one who can feel, know. I'm alone but not scared. It feels nice being inside myself. Better than walking up behind Mom at the stove, putting my nose in the fleshy back corner of her underarm, and taking a few deep breaths; better than laying my head on Daddy's big belly; better than peanut butter and jelly or Blue Bell's butter pecan ice cream or books or butterflies or tall pines—yes, the very sight of tall, skinny pines, with long necks like mine, makes me want to do a cartwheel and shout, "Thank you, God!" for teaching me how to reach and keep reaching. Even better than that.

"Do you know what time it is?" Mom says.

I have no choice but to open my eyes, join the outside world, and look at Mom standing in our doorway in her long, white robe. I know better than to not look at her while she's talking.

"If you don't get your butt out of that bed!"

I sit up and put my hand to my stomach. "My stomach hurts," I lie, and quickly pray, *Lord, forgive me.*

"Wait before you put those on," Mom says, walking over

to Naima, one leg already in her stockings. "Lift up your arm," she tells Naima, and sniffs her elbow. "Now your leg."

Naima barely lifts the leg with the stocking.

"I don't have time to play this morning. It's already eight fifteen. Sunday school starts in an hour."

Naima swings her arms overhead, grabs the wooden edge of the top bunk for support—ashy elbows in my face—and lifts her bare leg. As she tightens her grip to raise her leg higher, I notice her pointer finger peeling back one of the glow-in-the-dark heart stickers I've arranged in a perfect wave around the wooden frame of my bed. I push her finger over and press the yellow heart back down.

Mom grabs Naima's thigh and brings the knee to her nose. She has to do this with Naima because Naima likes to pretend-bathe—run water without getting in the tub, then put on lotion to hide her smell. But she always forgets to lotion her elbows and knees. Her elbows and knees always tell the truth.

Satisfied, Mom picks out Naima's dress, lays it on the bottom bunk, and looks up at me. "Do you feel like throwing up?"

"No," I say.

"Is your stomach cramping?"

"No."

"Have you had a movement this morning?"

I think about the many movements I've felt in my body this morning, but I know her kind of movement and my kind of movement are two different things and say, "No."

"That's the problem right there," she says. "Get up and try to have one. I'll be back." She walks out, hips switching underneath white terry cloth.

I climb down the wooden stairs on the back side of the beds and go to the bathroom, where I look for something different in the mirror. I just know, with all the motion, that there has to be a change, but I see the same gap between my two front teeth, the same long chin, and the same bubble lips. I lift my faded Snoopy nightgown above my breasts—same flat chest—and notice my breath raising my brown skin. I flood my lungs, watch my chest swell, and hold the air in, feeling my insides stir like glitter in a globe. I exhale and the tiny dots settle. I take another long breath, and the sparkles swirl and swirl deep beneath my skin in a place I don't know how to name, from where the songs in my head speak, from where tears race and eyes roll, from where gap-revealing smiles escape, laughter skips, cravings call . . . where words of love and fear whisper and scream, even if they never come out . . . the room inside the room inside the room.

"What are you doing in there?" Mom yells through the bathroom door.

"Nothing." I let down my nightgown and run water over my hands before I open the door. I know better than to have dry hands after supposedly trying to have a movement.

Mom waits in the hallway. Her hair is in a slick bun behind her right ear, but she's still in her robe.

"So?"

"No."

"Come on in here."

I follow Mom to the kitchen, where she makes me oatmeal with peaches and brown sugar on the stove. "Breakfast is ready," she yells, and the rest of the family comes in. We have breakfast together at the dining room table, but everyone else eats the good stuff: bacon, eggs, pancakes, and grits.

"Mmm-mmm-mmm, this bacon is good," Damon says, smacking. He has more on his plate than Daddy.

"Superb!" Daddy says in a lofty voice, and takes a sip of his orange juice with his pinky finger extended.

Naima giggles.

"These pancakes are something else," Damon says.

"Magnificent!" Daddy says.

"Great!" adds Naima. She's only nine, doesn't have many words waiting at the edge of her mind.

"I'm glad I'm not sick," Damon says.

"Why, I couldn't agree with you more," Daddy says.

"Eating oatmeal in the midst of all this good food would be a small tragedy."

"Worse than morning breath," Damon says, and everyone laughs, even Mom.

I want to join in, but I keep a straight face, stay committed to being sick so I can keep feeling my insides play.

After breakfast I pretend to try to have another movement. Again I wet my hands, and this time Mom is waiting outside the bathroom door in white stockings and a cap-sleeved, V-neck, navy blue dress that stops beneath the knee. She's put on her makeup—a thin, brown line on the lids of her slanted eyes and clear gloss on her thick, curvy lips. I doubt I can ever be such a lady.

"So?"

"No."

She makes me a mug of warm lemon water. I pretend again. When I open the door, a swirl of spices, citrus, and honey curls into my nose—Poison perfume, my favorite. Mom usually lets me dab a bit on my wrist for church, but I know better than to ask. For a moment I consider giving up my sick act so I, too, can smell pretty, but then she adjusts the white purse strapped to her left shoulder and shifts the black leather Bible in her right arm, and just like that, something inside me takes off running, something wild like excitement, no, desire, no, freedom, yes, freedom, flailing its arms and screaming, "No!"

"Have you lost your mind?" asks Mom.

"I'm sorry," I say in a voice sweeter than Poison. "But my stomach feels worse. I need to lie down." Another lie. And I would tell a hundred more to stay home, out of stockings and a dress.

"Go ahead."

I go back to bed, and Daddy convinces Mom she doesn't have to stay home with me. It's only a little stomachache . . . I'm old enough to be alone for a few hours . . . I can lock the doors and set the alarm . . . lie down and look at TV . . . be fine all by myself.

I watch them pull out of the driveway through the tall, narrow window flanking the front door, watch until I can no longer see Daddy's smoke-gray Volvo, watch until I know they are down the street, past the neighborhood pool, beyond the auto shop and corner store, and Daddy is looking both ways to cross Antoine. Once they cross Antoine, there's no turning back. Doesn't matter if someone forgets their Bible, or worse, forgets to put on deodorant—that's the rule.

I'm officially on my own.

I take off running toward anything calling my name. My first stop is the kitchen, where I open the spice drawer Mom always tells me to stay out of, and taste what I don't know: basil, sage, cilantro, cardamom, curry, and paprika. I take a whole bay leaf and carry it under my tongue into Mom and Daddy's room, where I spit it in the toilet, flush it, find Mom's perfume on the bathroom sink, and dab it on my earlobes, the U between my collarbones, and the knobs on my knees and big toes. I run to the living room, turn on the radio, and do the MC Hammer dance to gospel music. Even though it's hot outside and the air is on, I open every window in the living room, press my parted lips to each mesh window screen, and breathe the Houston heat. I unlock the back door, turn off the alarm, go outside, and lie down in warm, green blades under a blanket of September sun and stare at the violet dots sailing the red sea behind my closed eyes. I lie still, even when bugs crawl around my ankles and between my toes, perfectly still, moving farther inside the inside.

The tiny dots between my temples float higher and higher, then hover around the arch of my crown until I no longer feel alone. I enter the innermost room and lick the sweet peace of God—sweeter than all the Blue Bell ice cream in the world, sweeter than "Amazing Grace," nothing like the tasteless lessons I swallow during Sunday school.

I can't believe God has been right here, inside the inside, the whole time. Why hasn't anybody told me? I want answers:

*Where is Jesus? Heaven's gates? Am I in trouble for skipping church today?* But with every question I move farther out: room outside of room outside of room until there's nothing left to do but open my eyes. I try to close them, go back inside, but my thoughts and questions won't let me. Then I think maybe it's a sin to have tasted God and pray, *Lord, forgive me.*

I run back inside the house, lock the door, set the alarm, close the windows, brush the spices off my tongue, have a movement, take a shower (making sure to wash off the perfume), put on a clean set of pajamas, and turn on the television in the living room so I can easily pretend I've been nowhere, seen nothing but reruns of *The Cosby Show*, felt no One, tasted only the leftover breakfast Mom said I could reheat if I got hungry—been a good girl.

# Kickball on Christmas Eve

A gang of clouds is posted up in the Texas sky. But still I want my turn to kick the ball before the rain finds us outside my house on Bridge Forest Drive. "Dang, Naima, roll the ball!" I yell, standing in line behind Reina.

"Shut up, Taja!" Naima says, and rolls the red rubber ball straight down the wooden strip in the center of the street, right over home plate, a soft patch of green growing up through the concrete.

Reina runs to meet the ball, shy steps cut off by her long jean skirt. Skirts and dresses to play kickball, always, she and her little sister. Naima and I only wear them on Sundays, when I beg God to erase my sins from His long mind. My last sin, still sweet on my tongue, probably earned a million marks on the chalkboard of all He knows.

Reina kicks the ball with her shiny black shoe. "Foul," Naima yells out, and the ball travels to the right of first base, Reina's beige brick mailbox.

"Got it!" Theresa, Reina's little sister, yells, and runs to get the ball out of the shrubs beneath their front windows. Their curtains are open, but there's no Christmas tree decorated with lights, ornaments, and candy canes inside. Just nine fiery lights on the windowsill.

A hungry growl rolls through the clouds' dark bellies the same way one rolled through my belly before Reina offered me half the cookie she made at synagogue.

"At where?" I asked, sitting under her cedar elm during the bathroom break. We didn't need to pee.

"Synagogue," Reina said, breaking the blue star. "I put extra icing on this one."

"What's that?"

"Icing, you know, the same stuff you put on cake," and she licks a pointed end. Blue icing on the tip of her tongue.

"No, synagogue."

"Oh, it's the place we go visit God."

I knew she was talking about a different God, a wrong

God, a God against Christians' God, but the cookie called my name one too many times, and I held out my hand to receive two pointed ends of the star. I swiped my tongue over the icing—*Mmm, blueberry*—and ate it quick.

Naima rolls the ball again.

"Car!" yell Pam and her little sister Becky. They live next door, on the other side of the painted white fence that divides their yard from ours. They skip to the side of the street. Bounce, bounce, bounce goes their bushy blond hair. Not as bushy as Naima's and mine, but *still*. If I was a white girl with hair like theirs, I'd be mad.

Squeezing the ball between hip and elbow, Reina walks to her mailbox and takes her little sister's hand. The only time I hold Naima's hand is when we pray before meals. But sometimes at night I lean close to her little round nose while she's sleeping to make sure she's breathing. Helps me know I'm still breathing.

As the car inches by, Damon on the passenger side, the bass beats in my belly and chest. I don't know why all Damon's friends fill their trunks with speakers. I guess to be sure their hearts are still pumping. His friend drives an inch, brakes. Drives an inch, brakes—car humping the street. We laugh.

"Throw the ball at the car!" Naima shouts.

"Yeah, throw it! Throw it!" Pam, Becky, and I beg. But

Reina's too nice. Maybe it has something to do with her large, dark eyes. Long lashes like wings. Lids like halos. Hers and her sister's.

Damon and his friend park in the driveway and get out. They're still in their practice baseball uniforms. I grab the ball from Reina, run closer to the targets, and I'm about to hurl it at them when Damon's friend flinches and grins. Something about his grin, underneath the brim of his baseball cap, makes his face look sweet, makes me feel shy, and I drop the ball.

"Y'all better be glad I'm in the Christmas spirit," I say, trying to play it off.

Damon takes off chasing me, and I scream while running circles around the tree in our front yard until he catches me and tickles me (his favorite form of torture) in the grass.

"Help!" I yell.

Naima, Pam, and Becky run to my aid and start pulling on his arm, trying to get him to stop. Reina, Theresa, and Damon's friend just stand there and laugh.

"You're gonna make me pee! You're gonna make me pee!" I get out between laughs, and he stops.

"Keep messing with me and I'll tell Santa not to leave you any gifts tonight," Damon says, standing up.

"There's no Santa," Naima says.

"Everybody knows that," Becky chimes in.

"Yeah," Pam says, "only little kids believe in Santa, and we're not little kids." She pulls the sleeve of her shirt down to show off her bra strap.

Reina and Theresa both look away. Damon and his friend shake their heads.

*When did you get one?* I think. I hadn't noticed Pam's breasts getting bigger, but now I see two small bumps.

"Could've fooled me," Damon's friend says, and he and Damon exchange laughs before walking inside.

I should've thrown the ball at his head.


Reina kicks again. Another foul. Pam's yard. Closest, I run to get the ball from a bed of red begonias. It's tangled in white lights, the same white lights that trim the house.

"Pretty begonias," I said last Sunday in the driveway on the way to church—hair pressed, purple dress, looking out the car window, beyond the painted fence. "Why can't we plant begonias?" I asked my parents, mainly because I wanted to say *begonias* again.

Daddy looked out the window. Pam's dad mowed the grass. Pam's mom knelt in her red begonias with a watering can. Pam and Becky sat in jean shorts, petting their orange cat.

"We praise the Lord on Sundays," Daddy said, looking at me through the rearview mirror before backing out of the driveway. "We'd rather praise the Lord and go to heaven than work in the yard." He put the Volvo in drive.

*If God is everywhere, then why can't we praise God in our yard?* I wanted to ask but I knew better. I rolled down my window and waved to Pam, Texas's sweet December sun kissing my arm.

"A lot of good people go to hell. Only saved people go to heaven," Mom adds. *Saved. Confess with your mouth and believe in your heart. Believe.*

Lightning cracks the sky in the distance. I drop the ball back in the bed of red and white. *I believe.* Again, white lightning—a jagged slide from heaven to hell. *I believe.* I kneel in the bed, cool dirt holding my knees.

"Hurry up!" Naima shouts.

I move my hands through dirt, pretending to look for something lost. I close my eyes. No one can see this far.

*Please forgive me. I didn't mean to eat the cookie. Well, I did, but I didn't. It was calling my name—Taja—sounded sweet. When I licked the blueberry icing off the Hanukkah star, I felt something in me try to break free. I'm sorry. I should've gone to the bathroom with Naima at our own house. But I'm still young and I haven't gotten to the bottom of the difference between good, sweet, and saved; Christmas trees and candles; red begonias, no begonias; Sunday on either side of the painted fence. Please forgive me, God. Amen.*

The lightning stops. *Thank you, God.*

Another foul. Naima catches it. Reina's out.

My turn to kick the ball. It flies, a red star, down the street. I run. My laces flip, flop, trip up my lanky legs, but still I don't fall. First base. I hear the buzz that comes before the lights. Second. Lights on high metal poles stagger on, one by one, toward our end of the street. Third. So many clouds that we couldn't see the sky saying good night. Streetlights on: time for everyone to go home.

# Breathing Room

When I open our bedroom window in winter, Mom says, "Shut that window. It's too cold to be wasting all that heat." In the summer, she says, "Now you know good and well it's too hot to be wasting air." But I don't waste air. I take it into my nose, down my throat, and into my chest, where sometimes I hold it in, pull it deeper into my belly, down below my belly button, let it swirl, rise, and rush out. A few times, I've tried to teach Naima how to fill herself with air, but she just fills her cheeks—little brown balloons.

When Mom finally lets me open our window, air hurries to get out. Get out and go—that's all air wants to do. If it had a mom, she'd probably say, "You better sit your butt down somewhere." But it has no mom to tell it what to do. So it plays free. Flies outside, catches all the sounds, mixes them up like rainbow flecks in a twirling baton, and tosses them into our room: a pink box with barking birds, crying leaves, rustling music from cars one, two, three blocks away, chirping dogs, babies booming and booming and booming with bass, alive, until the air wants to run free again, and rushes out—whoosh!—trying to take everything with it. The bottom edges of our posters flip up, loose papers do front flips and somersaults, and our curtains kiss the window screen, breathing deeply (I can tell by the way the back side of the sheer white cotton rises and falls). My hair floats up off my shoulders, toward the opened window, and when I fill myself with air, my chest and belly travel forward, too, just a little. But I want to go far.

# Hungry Sunday

Sunday morning in March, before God picks up the sun, the Gulf of Mexico is like a ghost. After driving over an hour from Houston to get to the ocean, I can't even see it except for nine diagonal lines cast by the pier's light posts. Even then, I only see the parts that move: tiny waves, twinkling. I make a wish on the brightest wave, *Let my breasts grow big enough to need a bra*, say *Amen*—send it off to God, floating.

Along the pier, I walk beyond the first light. In the darkness between posts, the sound of the ocean makes me want to close my eyes, go back to sleep. We drive to Galveston early, when fish and crab like to eat. I'm usually hungry when I wake, too, but this morning I sipped orange juice and watched Naima and Mom split my pancakes, Damon take my bacon, and Daddy eat my eggs and grits. I didn't feel like eating.

Before breakfast, when everyone else was still asleep, I went into the kitchen, where I knew I would find Mom alone.

"What are you doing up?" she asked, and cracked an egg into a bowl. She was already dressed in her fishing clothes—khaki shorts and a long-sleeve button-up shirt.

"Can you buy me a bra?" I replied.

"No," she said, and whisked a mixture in a bowl.

"Why?"

"You don't need one." She dropped a bit of pancake batter onto the griddle on the stove to test if it was hot enough. The drop didn't sizzle.

"Look," and I arched my back, trying to make my breasts look bigger through my red Rockets T-shirt (my Snoopy nightgown had to go).

She whisked eggs in a different bowl.

"Look, Mom."

"I see, Taja," and she briefly turned to look at my chest. "When your breasts grow large enough to require a bra, I will buy you a bra. I promise."

I opened the fridge and got out the turkey bacon, hoping helping her cook would change her mind. "But girls at school already have bras," I said in the nicest non-talking-back voice I could find so early in the morning.

"Don't worry about what other girls have." She picked up the bowl with the pancake batter, tilted it over the griddle, and poured a perfect circle.

"But a bra is nothing." I found a pan in a bottom cabinet, placed it on the other side of the stove, poured some oil in it, turned on the burner, and waited for the pan to heat up. "Some girls wear makeup and shirts that show off their belly buttons. Some have multiple piercings and dye their hair all types of colors." *They also smoke cigarettes in the bathrooms, but I won't tell you that. Some girls even do nasty things with boys behind the temporary buildings after school, but you definitely don't need to know about that.*

"And?" Mom poured her last circle and got a black plastic spatula out of a drawer.

I placed a piece of bacon in the pan. It didn't sizzle. I turned up the fire. "I need *some* kind of cool factor."

"Cool factor?" she said, and lifted the edge of the first pancake she poured—golden brown. She flipped it and started on the rest. "Can you get the butter out of the fridge?"

I got Mom the butter and placed more bacon in the pan.

"Do you know Pam calls me her nerdy neighbor? On Friday I waved to her as I passed her down the hall, and I heard her say it to one of her friends. She barely even waved back."

"But y'all play together every day." Pancakes still on the grill, Mom began rubbing them with the stick of butter.

"Playing kickball at home is one thing, but at school she's too busy with her friends who wear bras and talk about the boys who like them to be friends with me. All I have to talk about are church and books. No boy has ever liked me. All I'm saying is the least I could do is wear a bra."

"You're not wearing a bra because Pam or anyone else is wearing one. You can't worry about what other people do. You have to do what's best for you."

"But wearing a bra is what's best for me," I said, forgetting about my nice non-talking-back voice.

"As long as you're in this house, your father and I will decide what's best for you," she said, pointing the stick of butter at me.

"So go to church and make good grades . . . that's all I'm supposed to do? So boring. I'm not a little kid anymore, Mom. When will I get to choose what I want to do?"

Mom looked at me like she wanted to slap me. She'd never slapped me before, but she often looked like she wanted to when I talked back too much. And I was way over the limit.

"Now that's enough, Taja. Go wake up your sister and brother and y'all brush your teeth and come in here for breakfast."

I did what I was told.

After unpacking the car, I carry the cooler for crabs, my arms stretched wide to hold the handles. With each step, my knees bang the cooler's side—underarms stretch, elbows stretch, wrists stretch—sloshing around the ice inside. Fingers stretch, slide. I put the cooler down on the wooden planks.

"Need help with that?" Daddy calls out.

I pick up the cooler. Knuckles stretch, and I walk fast to the third light post, where Mom likes to lower the crab nets. Up high, a swarm of bugs fight over the fluorescent light. They think it's the moon. Hungry for light, they think any light is the moon, but the moon is a thin-lipped smile. I follow the light from the post, out to the twinkling waves, and then to the water I can't see but know is there. I lean onto the pier's wooden rail, stare into the darkness, step up on the bottom rail—

"If you don't get your butt down from there!" Mom yells.

I step down and sit on the cooler. Naima drops two plastic grocery bags of food next to the cooler and plops down on the wooden planks. She forgets to look for bird crap. I see a small white pile between her ashy knees and point it out: "Ewwww."

Mom sets down the crab nets and a bag of raw chicken necks. "I have a feeling we'll be eating gumbo tonight."

"I don't know," Daddy says. "The wind is telling me different. The wind is saying something about fish. Fried fish, to be exact." He and Damon laugh, drop off Naima's and Mom's chairs, and keep walking, hauling their fishing gear to the ninth light post, where the water is deep. I don't need a chair. I go back and forth, stay in between.

Naima unfolds the chairs and arranges them so the nylon arms are touching. "Come on, Mommy. Sit down." She pats the seat of the chair, looking at me like I care.

"In a minute. Let me get us set up first," Mom says.

*That's what you get*, I tell Naima with twisted lips.

I know how to crab, but Mom likes to instruct me anyway: Tie the rope around the chicken neck. Tie it tight. Tie the chicken neck to the crab net. Make a knot. Loop the rope around the neck and through the net. Again, so the crabs can't claw off the neck. One more time, so there's no chance the crabs will claw off the neck. One more knot. Lower the net into the water near the beam. Steady now, so the net won't flip over. Tie the rope to the beam. Tie it tight. Good. Now we wait.

Here comes the sun! Over the Gulf of Mexico, God always picks up pink and purple before bringing gold along. I like to think He does this just for me. Same pink as my high-top Converse. Same purple as the grape bubble gum I chew.

Waiting for gold, I grow hungry and reach into the grocery bag for some plain Lay's.

"Did you clean your hands?" Mom asks, but I know it's not a question.

I reach for the hand wipes instead and snatch a wet cloth from the starry hole of the plastic cylinder. I wipe my hands—both sides—and reach for the Lay's again.

"I brought you a granola bar for breakfast."

"I don't want a granola bar," I say, bag of chips in hand.

"You know you only get one bag of chips. If you eat them now, that's it."

I open my chips.

Mom checks her net. "Three crabs!" She pulls up the net. "Open the cooler."

I get off the cooler but don't open it. I'm not about to wipe my hands again.

"Hurry! Open the cooler!"

Naima lifts the top.

Mom flips the net over the cooler, but the crabs hang on

with strong, shelled arms. Three jerks from Mom shake them off. Gray bodies fall. Flat legs, orange and blue, scramble over ice cubes. On all sides, crabs run into white walls. Claws stretch wide, reach, and strike the cooler's sides, trying to climb out.

Naima slams down the top and checks her net. "Four crabs!" she says, and pulls the net up, Mom's long chin over her shoulder.

Mom lifts the top, helps Naima shake off the crabs—all girls with orange legs—and shuts the cooler. "Check yours," Mom says.

"I'm not finished." I hold up my bag of chips.

Naima checks my net. No crabs. No chicken neck.

"I thought I told you to tie it tight," says Mom. She takes out another chicken neck, ties it on herself. "You want to lower it?"

"No, that's okay." I watch the net touch the ocean—water rushing into a ring of square snares—and disappear. *Can crabs see the net? Do they wonder what it is? Are they too hungry to think before they climb in? Do the crabs down there miss the crabs up here? Are they praying for their return?* I toss out a chip. Watch it float. Don't sit back down.

Daddy and Damon sit side by side. Poles straight, long lines stretched out to the sea. Daddy's line is stretched so far, it's invisible.

I open their cooler. Over ice and between silver cans of beer, fish with copper scales, white bellies, wet tails, and eyes like plastic stickers with black pupils that wiggle—except theirs are still. All lips parted, as if hoping to be fed, even dead.

"Hand me one of those, will you?" Daddy says.

"Yeah, me, too," Damon says, and smiles at Daddy. He plays it off like it's a joke but I know it's a test.

Daddy does, too, and looks over at Damon like, *Don't even try it.*

I reach in and out of the cold quickly and hand Daddy a beer, admiring the dirt under his fingernails.

"How are things up there?"

"Good, I guess. Probably caught twenty, twenty-five crabs so far."

"Shit!" he says, and sips his beer.

I love to hear Daddy curse. He doesn't curse around Mom. Sometimes he lets Damon curse, too, but only when the timing is just right. If it's wrong, then Daddy gives a warning: "That's two," as in almost three, and three is bad news.

I grab my pole from the wooden rail and sit on the cooler. Damon hands me the pail of shrimp. I take one, bait my hook, and cast my line into the sea—nowhere near Daddy's but not too far from Damon's.

I feel a tug and sit up. No, it's only a wave. I look at my watch: 10:46. Church just started. If I was there, I'd be sitting beside my friend Keisha. And on her other side would be Mona and Brandy, the twins I can't stand. We'd all be singing the first hymn. These are the only Sundays we ever miss church: hungry Sundays, Daddy calls them, when fish and crab are the hungriest. He weighs the weather and moon to tell. My favorite Sundays, when I don't have to put on a dress. But it's more than that. God seems closer over the Gulf of Mexico than He does in church. Like He's the salt I taste on my lips.

I feel a bite and a fish takes off running, making my rod arch and my line stretch invisible. I stand up.

"Looks like you've got a big one there," says Daddy.

I yank hard, trying to hook the fish like Daddy taught me. But my rod goes straight, and my line gets light. I reel it in. No fish. No shrimp.

"You've been feeding the fish good today," Damon says, and hands me a can of earthworms—soft-bodied Slinkys sliding in dirt. I lift one out and it curls around my finger, doesn't try to get away—poor thing has no brain.

"Need help with that?" Daddy asks.

"No, thanks," I say, and pretend to bait my hook, pretend

to scratch my leg as I let the worm go. Then I stand and sling my line into the sea as far as I can.

Sun thumps the back of my neck, and I'm hungry. I go back to the third light post to make a peanut butter and jelly sandwich. Before I clean my hands, I peek inside Naima and Mom's cooler. A pile of crabs, clawing. I'm about to shut it when one with orange legs climbs her way to the top. Climbs her way out. Scoots sideways all the way down the pier on skinny legs, claws clanking against the wooden planks. I walk beside her, listening to her scooting prayer. She scoots fast past Daddy and Damon, reaches the very end of the pier, leaps sideways over the edge, hangs in the air, and flips upside down. When she hits the water, I'm jealous. I want to leap, flip, and swim, too. But she sinks. Maybe I would sink, die, too. Then she moves—alive!—and disappears in the deep blue.

# The Sweetest Thing

Monday of the last week of school. As I sit down at my homeroom desk, I notice a sheet of wrinkled paper, torn from a spiral notebook, hanging from the desk's rectangular mouth. The side with the raggedy fringe is closest to me. I hate fringe. The spiral is there for a reason: to keep paper in. If you have to tear it out, at least get rid of the fringe.

Annoyed, I begin to slide the paper out, but it's heavy, weighed down by something. I lean over, peek inside the desk, and see a small, pink glass bottle. I grab it—a half-used bottle of perfume. I yank out the note, and written in all caps in red marker:

I LOVE YOU.

The air bloats around me. The classroom floats. A sweet, foreign fog covers me, and I close my eyes and run the fringe back and forth along my cheek. A boy loves *me*. Back and forth along my cheek. I feel new, like someone's waved a magic wand and made me beautiful.

But who?

I spy the boys still walking in, the boys getting settled at their wooden desks, the boys huddled in groups, rowdy with last-week excitement. I'm searching for a clue: eye contact, cracking knuckles, a cough, a shaking leg, a fumble of books, a bite of a bottom lip, too many blinks, too much cologne, a whistle, a whisper, a flinch, a naked and love-drenched face. Nothing.

Nothing in the halls.

Nothing at lunch.

Nothing at recess.

Nothing in line waiting on the big yellow bus to take me home.

At home I rush to my room and close the door behind me. Anxious to smell the perfume for the first time, I climb up on the top bunk and take the pink bottle of perfume out of the bottom of my backpack. The small glass bottle is round and covered with raised sections shaped like diamonds. I run my fingers over the diamonds and the grooves in between, and bring the little round hole in the silver plastic sprayer to my nose. Smells like candy.

"Hey." Naima barges in.

I quickly hide the perfume under my covers.

"What?" I say, annoyed.

"What's your problem? You playing kickball or what? Everyone's outside waiting."

*Should I go and show Pam? But she'll ask who it's from. That's the juiciest bit.*

"Hello, Earth to Taja."

"No."

"Why not?"

"I don't feel like it."

"Whatever." She slams the door behind her.

Alone again, I take the perfume out of its hiding place, squirt a teeny amount onto my pointer finger, and suck it. Bitter, but I roll it around on my tongue like chocolate and swallow. Another squirt on my finger before I put the perfume back in my backpack and lie down.

Lying on my back, I press my pointer finger into my chest and begin to write the possibilities. *B-o-b-b-y*, who sits behind me and annoyingly taps his foot on my chair. *A-d-a-m*, the only boy taller than me in class. *P-h-i-l-l-i-p*, who's always raising his hand with wrong answers to show off his deep voice. I can hear it now, echoing inside me—*I love you, I love you, I love you*. I stop writing.

I don't know who it is and I don't care. I'm not one of the pretty girls who boys act dumb around or give their lunch cookie to. I'm not one of those girls who huffs and puffs and flings her braids over her shoulder in annoyance with boys. Unless someone is making fun of the gap between my teeth or my height, I largely go unnoticed. But someone loves me.

I cross my hands over my chest and whisper, "I love you, too." And every atom in the air around me nods in approval.

Tuesday and I pretend to keep my cool. Keep my face washed of love while I sit at my homeroom desk, wondering who gave me the note and perfume. I'm wearing it—sprayed the liquid love a few times walking to the bus stop and did a twirl in its candy mist. I wish Pam could've at least smelled it, but her mom drives her to school every day.

"A zoo, this place," Danny says, and slides into his blue plastic seat in the first row beside me.

"Yeah, only four days left." I watch him as he takes out his red spiral notebook and writes the date in the upper right-hand corner, same as me. *Could he be?*

A tiny wad of paper hits Danny in the back of the head.

"Ms. Holmes," he yells, trying to tell. She doesn't look up from her magazine. "Why even bother," and he closes his notebook.

"I know," I echo, and close mine, too. And beautiful, shiny bells sound, drowning out the noise of the classroom. Danny is the only person in the class who reads faster than me. And I've never once heard him get stumped by a word.

Tapping his ballpoint pen on his desk (it's a clue . . . it's definitely a clue), he says, "You know, I was thinking—"

"Yes?" I want to remember this moment forever . . . him forever . . . his freckles . . . his red, curly hair . . . the way he neatly rolls up the edges of his T-shirt sleeves.

"Of running for class president next year."

*Huh?* And I attempt to fix my scrunched-up face.

"We could at least be watching a movie. Look at this," and he throws his hands up.

I look around at kids laughing and talking while sitting on top of their desks, at kids dancing, putting on makeup and nail polish, and throwing things. One kid is using a rubber band as a slingshot and little wads of paper weighted with spit as his ammunition—clever. It feels good . . . freeing, being in the middle of such chaos. "Yeah, a movie would be nice."

"Someone could get hurt!" His voice is high and loud. I

want to reach out and touch his skinny, freckled arm. I want to calm him so we can get to the part about love.

"If I was class president, this wouldn't happen, even in the last week of school. Everyone can still have fun without this kind of craziness. You know I'm right. All student council ever cares about are school-dance themes and spirit days. But this school needs more rules. And we would make the perfect team to help create them."

"We?" I'm really not interested in creating rules for other people to follow. I have enough rules to follow on my own.

"Yes, you could be my vice president. We can meet this summer to start organizing our campaign for next year."

*Now I see. You're still being shy. This is your way of trying to get close to me.* "Let's do it!"

We share smiles and raisins and campaign ideas. Then he writes my phone number in his red spiral notebook.

Before kickball, I ring Pam's doorbell.

She opens the door in a tank top, unaligned with her bra straps, and says, "Hey."

"Look what someone left in my desk yesterday," I say, and show her the letter. "I accidentally spilled half the perfume," I lie (can't have her thinking my admirer gave me a secondhand gift), and take the bottle out of the front pocket of my acid-washed jean shorts.

She snatches both from me. Sprays the perfume. "Nice. Who's it from?"

"Danny."

She looks up and to the left. "Danny?"

"Red hair . . . freckles."

"Oh, yeah. Danny!" she says, widening her eyes. "He's cute in his own way."

My insides want to scream in excitement of her approval, but I say, "Yeah, he's not too bad."

"Taja," Naima calls, and I take back my letter, quickly fold it, and put it in my pocket.

Pam slides the perfume into my pocket along with it.

"Thanks," I whisper.

"Y'all ready?" Naima shouts from the driveway. She already has huge sweat patches in the armpits of her pink shirt.

"Keep me posted," Pam whispers. "I want all the details."

"Okay," I say, smiling wide.


That night, Mom says it's too hot outside to cook. We can have whatever we can find. Hitting over a hundred degrees in May is much too much. The high heat could have at least waited until June.

I take strawberry Pop-Tarts to my room, half-lit by the evening sun, and climb into bed. Savoring the lingering sweetness, I imagine Danny beside me, touching my fingers and then holding my hand. My chest feels funny. As if it's swelled up to the size of the room, the size of the house. As if it's peeking through the roof, trying to bust out, float off— get carried away. A sharp ache in my teeth makes it shrink back down, makes me think of cavities. I consider getting up to brush them, but I don't want to let go. I let Danny hold my hand until the half-light is no light, let him carry me away again.

In the darkness, holding hands feels different. Floating has turned into a strange, warm aching down below. In the darkness, I remember that holding hands leads to kissing, which leads to touching body parts, which leads to sex. And sex before marriage is a sin. I let go. I try to sleep, try not to imagine Danny or feel the heat. But the heat is still there. I don't know how to put it out. I breathe deep. I open my eyes. Finally, I put my hands in prayer position and press them between my thighs.

Wednesday and I can't wait to see Danny. Can't wait to tell him how much I love him, but we need to wait on holding hands. He loves boundaries. I'm sure he'll understand.

I wait for him in the locker-lined hall outside of homeroom so we can talk privately. I watch him approach. Watch his bony knees glide smoothly underneath his khaki shorts. His knees look red, as if he was just down on them saying his prayers.

He's here and I've lost my words, my nerve.

"Hey, Taja," he says, red spiral notebook in hand.

"Hey, Danny," and I grab his notebook, open it, remove the pen stuck in the spiral binder, and write, *I love you, too.*

"What are you doing?" His small nose is crumpled up in annoyance.

"I love you, too. There, I said it. I love you, too. Now you can stop being shy and just say it already."

"I'm not being shy. I really don't—"

"Danny, stop. The perfume? The note? Student council? Meet me over the summer? Come on now."

"Perfume? I have no idea what you're talking about. If we're going to work together, we can't have any of this funny love business." His voice is cold . . . his big, reddish-brown eyes bare . . . no funny love there.

"You're right, excuse me," and I take off toward the girls' bathroom, where I stay until I hear the warning bell . . . where I remember seeing Danny cry when his mom dropped him off the first day of school . . . where I realize I don't love Danny anyway.

Thursday and nothing. No one. I'm beginning to think the whole love-note thing is a big joke. But I still spray the perfume and do a twirl in its candy mist on my way to the bus.

After school, I lie and tell Pam that Danny has bad breath. That there's no way I could imagine kissing him if he has bad breath. And there's no point in having a boyfriend if you can't even imagine kissing him. It's going nowhere, Pam agrees, and promises someone else will come along.

Friday and Flatulent Freddie whistles loudly at me as I step off the bus. His face is small, but his nose is huge, as if God made it so he can fully smell himself.

"Taja!" He's standing beside a group of kids, probably either farting or trying to fart. He loves making people suffer with his sickening smells.

"Yes?" but I walk straight toward school, don't want to get too close.

"Wait up," and he hurries to catch up. "Did you . . . get . . . I mean . . . like . . . my gift?" His face is as pink as the bottle of perfume.

*You? I can't love you.* "Yeah, who doesn't like candy?" and I smile, try to keep things light, away from love. But I can already see it in his eyes, something hungry, something sweet and soft I don't want to hurt.

"Sorry it was only half full. It was the best one I could find on my sister's dresser."

"That's okay."

"Excuse me for a second." He walks away, circles a group of people, and comes back with a rotten smell trailing.

I back up. "Sorry, Freddie, but I don't love you."

"But why?" His face moves from frantic to sad.

"I already love someone who goes to my church," I lie.

A hard swallow and lowered eyes.

To cheer him up, I think of a plan. And after the first bells rings, I twist the top off the bottle of perfume, hide it in my hand, and walk slowly around homeroom pouring it out. Kids ask each other, "What's that smell?" Say it's making them sick. The teacher puts down her magazine and asks who did it again and again. Everyone looks at Freddie, confused, wondering if a fart could smell so sickly sweet. As I slide into my seat, Danny is the only one looking at me, looking like he suspects, like he's ready to tell. So, I open my hand and show him the empty bottle. It's the last day. Who cares?

# Freestyle

I let go of Mom's hand and walk through the crowd toward a painting of a girl in a yellow dress, kneeling at a fountain— eyes closed, head bowed, hands cupped, catching water from above. Drinking or praying? Maybe both. Yes, in a painting, anything is possible.

In the painting beside her, there's a jazz scene: big, round cheeks blowing brassy horns. I wonder if the girl can hear the music, if it sounds the same as here in Hermann Park. Lively rhythms from the band onstage blare through tall, black speakers, making me wish I had a Hula-Hoop. I bet the women around here can hula-hoop good by the way they're moving their hips to the beat—jamming on Juneteenth, celebrating being free. Mom can hula-hoop even better than me.

Wait—where's Mom? Daddy? At least Naima's still here, holding my hand. She's staring at a wooden naked woman.

"Come on. Let's go," I say.

"No," Naima whines, and touches the woman's carved, ebony breasts.

I rejoin the moving crowd, holding Naima's wrestling hand as tight as I hold my fishing pole while reeling in a squirming hardhead. In Galveston, I always throw the hardheads back, but you can't pick your sister like you pick your fish.

Ahead I see a tall woman with strong, bronze shoulders. Her hair is held up by an oval leather barrette with a wooden stick running through it.

"Mom!" I yell, dragging Naima faster, weaving and squeezing through the crowd. "Mom!" I call out again, reaching for her shimmering shoulder, but my hand doesn't make it as high as I want. I accidentally swipe the side of her breast, and a young, pretty stranger whips her head back, narrows her round eyes, looks me up and down, once, twice, and turns away.

I stop and Naima walks my left shoe off my heel. I shuffle us out of the crowd, standing on my tiptoes and turning my head in every direction, before fingering my Converse back on.

"Are we lost?" Naima asks, digging in her ear.

"Stop that." I slap her probing hand.

"Ouch!" she says, and rubs the wax between her first finger and thumb.

"Gross," and I pull her closer.

"Can I have some ice cream?" she says, pointing past me.

I feel the cold on the back of my thighs, turn, and see three huge tins of ice cream—all brown     inside a silver cart. I wonder why chocolate is the only flavor. A skinny old man with a large mole on his forehead stands behind the cart. He has watery blue eyes, just like Gigi, my great-grandmother. She probably has him beat on age, but if she were here, she would still probably try to flirt. Gigi flirts, curses, smokes, and generally says and does whatever she wants. I love it. Mom hates it.

The old man is wearing a T-shirt with a black-and-white picture of two old, bearded men leaning on hoes in a field the shape of Texas, the words *"A Celebration of Freedom"* printed beneath. I imagine the old men grunting, sweating, and struggling to loosen the earth under the orange June sun, and then after hearing the news of slavery being over (two and a half years late), singing, running, and hurdling a high fence.

I could take off running, too. Mom isn't around to tell me to sit my butt down. But which way would I go? There are so many paths to choose. I could take a wrong turn, and just like that, Naima and I could be lost forever. Oh, how I would miss the pretty little sandwiches waiting for me after school each day, the proud wrinkle on the bridge of Mom's nose when I show her my grades, the way Daddy's belly jiggles when he laughs at his own jokes at the dinner table, the feeling of floating when he picks me up from the sofa, carries me down the long hall, and lifts me all the way up to the top bunk, where I lie still as the flesh in the middle of my forehead waits for his kiss good night.

"Well, can I?" Naima says, yanking my arm.

I dig in the pocket of my jean shorts, hoping to find a few forgotten dollars. The man behind the cart puts a scoop of chocolate on a waffle cone and hands it to a young girl wearing two French braids, same as Naima's and mine, except ours end with black rubber bands, hers with purple plastic barrettes. The girl licks the chocolate, already melting in the hot sun, while the woman standing behind her pays the man. I wish I had a bill in my pocket to buy Naima a cone, to make her forget I let go of Mom's hand and led us astray. But I say, "You don't need any ice cream."

"But—"

"But nothing. Come on," I say, in my most Mom-like tone, and lead her away from the cart, into the crowd. *We* have to make it back to the place I let go of Mom's hand. She'll be there waiting. I know she will.

With a sea of people moving toward us, I feel as if I'm swimming against a strong current, fighting to take each stroke, to hold onto Naima. I look back to make sure she's not scared and see the curve of her little round nostrils flaring—good, she's still mad. I angle my body to the side, trying to slide through the crowd, but waves of people close in on me even more. I turn to the front and take strong strokes, extending my legs to take up every inch of empty space and looking people dead in the face to let them know to get out of my way. There! Ahead I see the painting of the girl at a fountain hanging above the crowd on a wall in a tall, white tent. I lengthen each stroke, stepping into taken space, bumping people's shoulders. Here! This is where I let go.

I stand on my tiptoes and jump up and down; Naima does the same even though her head never makes it above the crowd. I wave my arms high above my head and yell, "Mom! Daddy!" just in case they're close enough to hear, but no one comes running. My legs weaken. Beads of panic swarm in my belly, fill up my chest, but I brace myself and take a deep breath.

"Don't worry. We'll find them," I say, with a happy face.

But the tears hanging from the thick row of lashes on

Naima's bottom eyelids say she doesn't believe me.

To cheer her up, I lead her out of the crowd, along the row of vendors, past African fabric; baskets; earrings; beaded necklaces and masks; paintings; stained glass like the butterfly thermometer stuck to our bedroom window; slabs of ribs and brisket, burgers, breasts, and wings, sizzling over a fire on metal bars in thick smoke smelling spicy-sweet; drawings of Martin Luther King; and drums people beat fast between their knees. But Naima doesn't try to touch anything. *Think, Taja, think. Where could they be?*

Just before I let go of Mom's hand, I remember her saying something to Daddy about a hill. Is this a hill we are standing on? I look back behind the vendors, where three women sit on a slope beneath a live oak, braiding each other's hair. The earth is definitely higher here than down there, in front of the brown, tent-shaped theater, where people sit shoulder to shoulder, clapping to a gospel choir singing onstage. But it's lower than over there, on the other side of the audience, where people sit on blankets. *That's it!* She wanted to lay our blanket on the hill.

"I know where they are," I tell Naima, and head toward the hill, walking around the vendors and the crowd. Under the shade of live oaks and tall pines, we shorten our strides and pump our free arms for speed. But my right arm wants to pump, too. Plus my palm is sweaty from holding Naima's hand for so long, so I let it go. As soon as she's free, she tries to pass me. We race, rocking our hips and locking our knees like the speed walkers on TV. With the help of my long legs, I'm winning. Wait, Naima's pulling ahead.

"Stop cheating!" Both of her new high-top sneakers keep leaving the ground at the same time.

"I'm not!"

I pull ahead again, but I can't see Naima in the corner of my eye, so I slow down, but not too much—don't want her strong legs passing mine. As I step out of the trees, into the last of the crowd, I see a stream of water, shining with the light of the sun. "Look!" I say, pointing to a huge, silver fountain at the top of the hill. I take off running. Naima quickly passes me. I try to catch up, but there's just not enough power in my legs to lift and lower my feet that fast.

Naima stops at the fountain and reaches her hand in the arched stream of water pouring from a titled bowl suspended from the silver woman's chest. No breasts for Naima to touch, only flat, simple shapes and empty spaces: a cut-out diamond for a face that reveals a pretty little piece of blue sky; radiating spikes for hair like the Statue of Liberty's crown; a round hole for a torso that shows shifting white clouds; and, for arms, two solid triangles, extending from her shoulders to the tops of her legs, giving the impression of her posing with her hands on her hips. How grand she looks standing at the top of the hill. Like she's been there for a thousand years.

"Beat you!" Naima says as I stroll up, pretending I wasn't trying to win.

"So," I say, and outdo her by taking off my shoes and climbing into the shallow pool that surrounds the tall, silver lady. My head only comes to the pointed tips of her elbows.

Naima steps up onto the short stone wall and jumps into the water with a big splash, her new shoes still on.

I ignore Naima (she hates that) and walk through the turquoise water, cool wetness washing against my calves, cold coins shifting beneath my feet. I pick up a copper penny with my long toes, make a wish—*Next time, let me win*—release it, and watch Lincoln's raised face sink.

"Look!" Naima says, standing under the woman's bowl, water pouring over her head. "I'm washing my hair."

I take three leaps, stand in front of Naima, and make a bowl with my hands to catch the water above her head. "So, I'm washing my hands."

She cups her hands and raises them higher than mine, and I lift mine as high as they will go. Even on her tiptoes, she can't reach my hands anymore. "No fair," she says, and sits down in the pool.

The water flows off my palms, down my outstretched arms, and wets my chest and belly, sprinkles my cheeks and neck. In the stream, shards of conjoined color—purple and pink, yellow and green—course through streaks of brilliance. I lower my hands, step closer, and feel the color prickling my skin, even closer, and allow myself to be immersed in the bright lights. With my eyes closed, the water beats the crown of my head, one and two and three and four, and cuts my mind wide open. I see color everywhere, taking all shapes, all sizes—blending and twisting, then stacking and crumbling, then bubbling, multiplying, and blasting—all types of liberties.

When the beating stops, I look up. Naima's hands cup over my head, and only a golden ray of water streams through. I lift my chin, open my mouth, and stretch out my tongue—tastes like the water in the neighborhood pool, but I swallow it and let my insides dive in, swim freestyle. Then I fold my legs beneath me, feeling the cool water rush up my jean shorts and over the curved bones of my pelvis.

"I bet you can't do this." Naima lies in the water, floating facedown like a dead woman. Loose strands from her French braids float on top of the water, looking scarier than the black veins beneath my tongue.

I want to scream *Stop!* and pull her up, but there's no way I'm letting her know she's creeping me out.

She sits up, gasps for air, and pushes her hair off her sun-browned face. "Your turn."

"That ain't nothing. What about this?" I say to disguise my fear, and crabwalk backward, adding a high kick each time I take a step. With my leg reaching for the sky, strong hands grab me under my shoulders. I'm in the air, screaming, "Put me down!" and then on my feet, watching Mom snatch up Naima and bring her to the ground.

"Have y'all lost your minds?" Mom grabs our arms, long fingernails digging into my skin, and swings us together in front of her.

"But we were looking for—"

"*Shut up!* I don't want to hear a *single* word come out of your mouth. Do you have *any* idea how worried I was?" she says, squeezing our arms and shaking us each time she stresses a word. "Do you have a *clue* of what could have happened to you? And to find you *playing* in water in your good clothes and shoes!" Spit flies from her tight lips. A fat vein in her long, slender neck sinks and rises like a stream of raging waters. "Oh, yeah, y'all have lost your minds all right, but I bet you find them when we get home. I can't *wait* to get you home." She yanks us and starts walking, still holding our arms, wringing our skin.

"Ouch!" Naima cries, arm in the air, trying to twist out of her grip.

People turn their heads and stare, but Mom couldn't care less. She snatches Naima's arm back down before squinting at me, then Naima, me, then Naima. "It took me *eight* hours yesterday to wash and press all that hair."

My arm stings and throbs, and I'm certain as soon as we get home, Mom will whip us until Daddy tells her to stop, but somehow, I'm trying to keep my lips from cracking a smile. I yank down their corners, but they break free and curl up, higher and higher, unafraid of Mom's anger. Inside me, there's no space for fear. Everything is still brimming with bright lights, flowing, pulsing, bubbling, and dancing—unbound.

*She felt an answer seeking her,*

*but where? When? How?*

—Zora Neale Hurston,
*Their Eyes Were Watching God*

# Solo

Lately I've been carrying around a picture in my mind of a girl in church singing a solo. She looks like me, but a different me, a better me. Her forehead is smaller, her hair is longer, and there's no gap between her two front teeth. She stands wearing a purple T-shirt, matching Converse, and holey jeans before pews and pews of shiny shoes, wide-brim hats, polyester, ruffles, cuff links, and pleats.

She sings with her eyes closed. She sings with her whole soul. (I can tell just by looking at her.) Her song is a prayer and God hears her. But I can't hear her song. It's like a secret between her and God. Even when I get still . . . so still . . . even stiller . . . still until my nostrils tremble, I only hear uneven sounds mixed up with pieces of prayer—a broken song.

That's why tonight I'm trying out for a solo in next Sunday's service. I've been singing in the choir since I was five but never tried out for a solo. Never thought my voice was special enough to stand alone. It doesn't climb high like a soprano or swing low like a tenor. I'm just an ordinary alto.

But the girl in my mind is an alto, too. I know because she doesn't look stuck-up like a soprano. And she definitely doesn't have a voice deep enough to be a tenor. That would be weird, and she doesn't look weird.

Now I'm sitting in the choir stand, waiting to audition, wearing an outfit just like hers. My friend Keisha is sitting to the right of me on the second pew. She's an alto, too. To my left is George, the new boy, the only boy brave enough to own his high pitch and sit with the girls. The rest of the boys, half of whose voices are higher than mine, declare tenor on the third row. And, of course, sopranos sit on the first.

"Okay, everyone . . . settle down, please," says Ms. Mason, the youth choir director. "Quiet, please." She's sitting at the piano at the bottom of the steps in work clothes, dark panty hose, and purple slippers. "Quiet!" And she holds her pointer finger down on the piano's far left key until the low note swallows all sound in the sanctuary. She releases the key.

"Now, show of hands for those trying out for the first song."

George raises his hand.

"George." Ms. Mason nods, her straight, stiff hair, flipped up at the ends, briefly leaving her shoulders.

He puts his hand down. Mona and Brandy, the pastor's twin daughters, who sing a duet almost every Sunday, who have off-white skin and true brown eyes the same color as their long hair, and whom all the boys love, look back at George from the first pew and start exchanging whispers. Mona begins to raise her right hand—*yes, please choose this song*—but Brandy snatches it down. They exchange harder whispers.

"Anyone else?" asks Ms. Mason.

Mona whips her head away from Brandy, making the tip of her long braid swipe my knee, peeking through the hole in my jeans, and folds her arms in defeat. Keisha nudges me with her elbow, and I think about raising my hand so I won't have to face off with the duo.

"You can beat him," Keisha whispers in my ear.

I know I can, but the chorus of the first song has *blood* in it, and I don't want my first solo to be about blood. Keisha may not understand this, so I whisper, "He's new. It would be his first solo, too."

"So? Don't want to upset your boyfriend?"

I laugh. "You mean *your* boyfriend." Although I always toss George back when Keisha throws him my way, I secretly love his thick lips and thick brows and sunken eyes, surrounded by lashes running wild.

"Congratulations, George. 'Nothing But the Blood' is yours," Ms. Mason says, and jots down something in a notebook sitting on top of the piano. After a few moments, she presses a white key with a bright note and writes something else, then a higher note and writes, and an even higher note and writes.

Behind me a boy hurls, "Way to go, Georgette," in a girl's voice. George doesn't turn around, keeps his hands folded in his lap. Then, in an even higher tone, "Yeah, awesome, Georgette." And someone else, "Hey, Georgette, can't wait to see you in your pretty dress."

Giggles upon giggles and I turn my head back, first this way, then that, and roll my eyes until they hurt.

"Quiet," Ms. Mason calls out without looking up from her notes.

"You did good," I whisper to George. But as soon as the words leave my mouth, I feel stupid. *What am I talking about? He didn't even have to try out.*

I feel something graze my knee and look down to see George's right hand land on my thigh. My insides grip in surprise, grip at his touch, at this feeling—pulsing and rising and pulsing and rising up from a low, untouched place. The heat, the sweatiness of his fingertips come through the hole in my jeans, and then it's gone. I watch as his right hand floats back over my thigh, the space between our legs, his thigh, and to his left hand. Watch as if I can will his hand, his fingers to come back and touch me again.

Keisha nudges me. "Ooh, I saw that. Looks like somebody's got a boy—"

I dig my elbow into her ribs until she shuts up. I hope George didn't hear that.

"Show of hands for the second song," says Ms. Mason.

Mona's and Brandy's right hands shoot up at the same time, flashing the same hot-pink polish on their nails.

"Duet, right?" asks Ms. Mason.

"Yes," in unison, and after they lower their hands, Brandy glances back at George with an irritatingly sweet smile on her face.

I glance at George and catch his lips spreading. *What are you doing? Don't smile at her.*

"Anyone else?" asks Ms. Mason.

Keisha knocks her knee into mine.

I glance back at George. He's still smiling.

"Well, if there's no one . . ."

Keisha lifts up my arm and it flops back down. "Taja!"

she whispers hard, and lifts up my arm again until my wrist points toward heaven. I take the weight of my arm and raise my hand.

"Are you and Keisha trying out for a duet? Or do you want a solo?" Ms. Mason asks.

Mona and Brandy are staring dead at me—their eyes squeezing my throat, threatening to steal my voice. But I want my solo.

"Solo," I say, but the sound is very small.

"Speak up, child."

"Solo," I say louder.

"Okay," and she nods. "Let's hear you first."

"Yeah, let's hear you," says Brandy, and she smiles at George again.

George's smile is even wider than the last time. It's the same stupid grin all boys give to Mona and Brandy—nostrils flared, full row of upper teeth showing. It's like they all read the same handbook for looking as stupid as possible. I can't believe I let him touch my leg. I can't believe I thought he . . . I can't sing in front of him. I can't let him hear me talk to God. But maybe hearing my voice might make him love me, not her. Love. I look at his folded hands and wonder if that's what I felt when he touched me. Love. I search the creases in the skin of his folded fingers. I search myself. But all I find is fear, flapping its frantic wings inside me, all around me.

Keisha pats my leg. "You got this."

I snatch her words and press the triangular tips of my shoulder blades extra hard against the wooden pew as I stand up, trying to feel something else, and scoot fast past Keisha and the altos, to the microphone stand at the end of the pew. Looking out at the sanctuary's rows and rows of empty pews, I imagine them packed, waiting to hear my solo, and I wish I could go sit back down. But I can't. *Can I? No*, so I stop looking at the pews and stare at the stained-glass windows on the sanctuary's right side, lit up from behind by the lights in the parking lot.

Behind me a boy coughs, "Flat booty," and the other boys laugh.

I want to grab a hymnbook from the rack on the back of the sopranos' pew and throw it at someone's head, but I keep my eyes focused on the stained glass.

"Quiet!" Ms. Mason shouts. "Go ahead, Taja. Just try singing the chorus."

*Did I hear George laughing with the boys?*

Ms. Mason clears her throat, and my eyes find a bright blue pane to look into, deep, deeper.

"Come on, Taja," Keisha says, and I try to imagine myself as the girl I've been carrying around in my mind. I close my eyes and see blue. I'm the girl on a pier over the ocean, long toes gripping planks, slowly letting go. She jumps, but I'm not ready. Maybe she wasn't ready either because now she's sinking. I start singing.

*"He's all over me."*

Now we are both sinking, and my voice is cracking under the weight of George's hand on my thigh . . . George's smile at Brandy . . . hearing God . . . the hope of love. *Where are you, God? Flat booty . . . flat booty . . . flat booty. Can't you hear me, God? Flat booty. Stop laughing at me.* I try to swim back up.

*"He's keeping me alive."*

But I can't swim. I can't find my voice, my limbs. Everything seems to be lost down here.

*"He's in my hands. He's in my feet."*

I'm mouthing the words but I don't know if they're coming out. I can only hear silence . . . a dazed, boy-made silence I don't understand. Somehow boys and God are getting all tangled up. *But what do boys have to do with God?*

"You can be seated, Taja."

The sanctuary is silent. Keisha tries to smile, but she can't bring her slanted eyes to meet mine. I sit down and Mona and Brandy don't even turn around. George doesn't move his hands, still folded in his lap. *I'm so embarrassed.* Heat rises behind my eyes—*no, that would only make me look worse*—and

I focus on playing with the strings hanging from the hole in my jeans.

Mona and Brandy sing a perfect duet. Don't know how they can be so nasty and still hear God so clearly.

Ms. Mason announces that George, Mona, and Brandy will sing at the celebration on Sunday, dismisses the choir, and asks to speak to me. I let everyone clear out of the sanctuary before I stand up and make my way to the bottom of the stairs.

"Have a seat," she says, and pats the empty space beside her on the black padded piano bench.

I sit down. I can't look at her, so I stare at the keys and fight the urge to press the white key farthest to the right.

"I don't want you to get discouraged."

I need to hear a high note.

"Many people struggle the first time they sing in front of people."

The highest note.

"It takes a lot of guts to—"

I press the key and it sings. I hold it down until it fills me. "Thanks," and I get up and run away from my solo, out the left side door of the sanctuary.

When I step outside into the courtyard, a bright light comes on and shines in my face. This is usually where everyone waits for their parents to get out of Bible study, but it's empty except for the hot July air buzzing with something wild . . . a song . . . no, a chant. I follow it away from the motion-sensored lights to the back of the sanctuary.

"Go, go, go," comes from a crowd of kids gathered around something I can't see. No motion-sensored lights back here, but the full moon shines bright on my little sister's bushy ponytail. She's standing with her friends, who'd rather attend youth Bible study than sing in the choir. *No, thank you.* She's chanting, "Go, go, go," with everyone else. Even Keisha, who's standing behind my sister, is chanting. I make my way to the front of the crowd and see George facing Brandy, holding her hands, dangling the possibility of a kiss above everyone's hungry faces. "Go, go, go." George notices me—my heart drops a few inches in my chest—then he looks back at Brandy.

"Do it if you're gonna do it," Mona says.

Brandy reaches out her lips, and George meets her lips with his. They kiss and kiss, tongues tangling and untangling between mouths opening and closing. Hoots and hollers and my heart stings like someone is pinching and twisting it, hard, even harder. High fives to George, a circle of squeals around Brandy, and tears rise up behind my nose and eyes. I run away before they can escape.

Back in the bright light, I lie flat on my back in the

grass, arms stretched out like Jesus. I do this so I can feel the overgrown blades against my skin—an itch I don't scratch. The only thing keeping the tears back. The harsh light in my face, and the sweet itch digging into the back of my arms and neck, numb this night that has beaten me. But when I get too still, the motion-sensored light forgets I'm here. I move and it remembers. Move and it remembers. Move and it remembers until I'm tired of moving and I lie still—forgotten, forgetting.

# In the Middle

"**S**top it," I say to Naima, and put my foot back in front of hers.

"You stop," she says, shoves me, and gets back in front.

We're waiting in the hall, outside of the door to Gigi's new apartment. Her old house was way better. The new place reminds me of the hospital I once visited with Mom when Sister Collins from church got sick. Pale yellow halls full of sick, yellow smells.

"Seriously!" I shove Naima so hard, she almost falls.

"Enough," Mom says through clenched teeth, and yanks our arms. "Both of you behind Damon."

I look back at Damon, standing behind Mom and Daddy, and he widens his eyes at me. Then I look at Daddy . . . his eyelids look heavy, sad.

"Now!" Mom says.

But Gigi's door starts to slowly open, and Mom clutches our shoulders so we stay in place.

When Gigi finally opens the door, my chest tightens. Her pink housecoat swallows everything but her wrists and ankles. Baby wrists and ankles without the softness or plumpness.

"Hi," Mom says cheerily, and gives her a hug.

I stand there, afraid to move, imagining myself wrapping my hand around her wrists to see if my thumb could reach my knuckles.

"Hi," Naima says, and hugs her, too.

Then I notice something suspicious about my knuckles. As if I'm old like her, and all the years are hiding inside the wrinkled dimes in the middle of fingers. The hump in her back, her thinness, her mothball scent—maybe they're all mine, hiding.

Damon pokes me hard in the back and I step forward. Afraid to touch her, I bend my tall, lanky body over her and pat her back with one hand.

"Hello, Taja," she says.

"Hi," I say, but it doesn't feel like I'm speaking to Gigi. This can't be Gigi.

When I pass her kitchen, a strange food smell mixes with the mothball scent and makes me nauseous. I walk into the living room and sit on her plastic-covered sofa with Naima and Damon while Mom and Daddy sit with her at her dark wood dining table—eight sides like a stop sign. I only have two sides, one in and one out.

August, and Gigi has the heat on. It's hot as hell. *Maybe hell is hiding.* I quickly close my eyes. *Lord, forgive me for all my sins on both my sides. Amen.*

"Let me check it out," Daddy says to Mom, and gets up. "Maybe she forgot to turn it off." He finds the thermostat on the wall near the kitchen and moves the switch at the bottom. "There, it should cool down soon."

But not soon enough. I'm still nauseous and hot. Damon pulls his T-shirt to and fro, Naima fans herself with her hand, and I try both. Neither works, so I put my head down between my knees. No air. Can't breathe. Mom walks over to the glass balcony door, slides it open, and motions for me to step outside. The backs of my bare thighs peel away from the plastic as I stand. Tiny streams of sweat trickle down the backs of my knees to my socks, two pairs—purple and pink—scrunched and stacked to set off my purple Converse.

Outside on her balcony, there's standing room only. No room for her rocking chair. Each time we'd visited her in Tennessee—once every summer for as long as I can remember—she liked to spend the evenings smoking her long, skinny pipe, rocking in her white wooden chair. Daddy would sit for hours at her feet. How many times would the floorboard creak? Guess and count—Naima's and my game. Usually one rock, two creaks, but sometimes she'd rock halfway and stop before the creak, or rock all the way forward and cause another creak, to throw us off.

I look over the railing. A cement path snakes through grass and stops at a thick patch of trees in the distance. The sun screams orange as it sinks into the untamed green. Along the path, old people roll in wheelchairs, walk with canes, and sit on benches. An old lady with a bright yellow scarf waving from her head and a cigarette hanging from her mouth tries to roll her wheelchair into the thick green. She's almost there when I see a man in a white uniform running to stop her. My insides root for her: *Go, old lady, go*, but the man catches her and wheels her back.

The patio door slides open and Damon sticks his head out. "Time to come back in. Gigi cooked," he says.

I stare at the open door. I don't want to go back in.

"It's just Gigi, Taja," he whispers.

*No, it's not.* It's not the same Gigi who lets me try on lipsticks at the mall or stay up half the night watching black-and-white movies with her or "taste-test" chocolate candy from the bins at the grocery store or who once even let me take a sip of her gin (it was disgusting, but still).

Damon steps outside and slides the door closed behind him. "She's sick," he says, and leans his elbows on the railing beside me. "She has cancer."

*Cancer . . . cancer . . . cancer*—the word echoes inside me.

"And she's too old to do anything about it."

"Why didn't anyone tell me?" I turn to look at him, but he's looking out at the distant trees. Tears form in my eyes and one rolls down my cheek. I angrily wipe it off and look down.

Damon steps closer to me so our elbows are touching. "Daddy didn't think she would be this bad. He didn't want to ruin the trip."

"But he told you," I say, and chip at the rusty paint on the railing with my fingernail.

"I'm the oldest. He knew I could handle it."

"I'm not a little kid anymore." I dig my thumbnail underneath a large section of peeling black paint and flick it off. A cloud of powdery red rust rises and falls.

"Well, look how you're acting."

Another flick . . . more red rust.

"Gigi's just old," he says, softly.

I stare at the railing . . . at the black paint peeling . . . the red rust underneath, taking over.

"We need to go back in," and he takes his weight off the railing.

I follow him inside.

Mom is at the dining table, preparing plates with small portions. She's removed her blouse, and her camisole clings to her large chest. Her oval face is dripping with sweat. "We'll only be able to have a taste because we just ate dinner," she says—the only lie I've ever heard Mom tell.

Daddy brings our plates to us on the sofa. The smallest amount of food goes to Naima, and I'm jealous. She's only two years younger than me, but she has three green beans and I have seven. It's not proportionate. Plus, Damon is three years older than me and we have the same amount. It's not fair.

I taste a green bean—mushy, flavorless. I swallow the rest of them without chewing. Try to do the same with my chicken, but the first piece gets stuck halfway down my throat. Damon bangs on my back to dislodge it, a little harder than necessary, but I don't get mad because I get out of eating the rest of my chicken.

"Sorry, I must have baked it too long," Gigi says.

"No, it's my fault," I say. *I should have chewed my chicken.*

I spot a picture of me on top of the TV, which is playing *Sanford and Son*. I'm smiling with my lips pressed together. Beside me is a picture of Naima with a gap bigger than mine, but she displays hers proudly. I stand up to see the rest of the photos. I know everyone in color, but when the reds, blues, and greens fade, I have trouble. In antique brown, a beautiful woman in a veil poses with a man in a pin-striped suit, the slope of her high cheek resting against his meaty chin. In black and white, a woman sits in a chair, brushing the right side of a pretty girl's parted hair; the left side is already braided, hanging over her shoulder to her ribs.

In front of the pictures lies a long suede bag, browned by time and beaded with bright blue stars. Fringe borders the bag. The tiny turquoise beads call my name, and I clasp my hands behind my back. *Look, don't touch.* They keep calling (turquoise is my favorite color), and I send my eyes to their far left corners to see if anyone at the grown-up table is looking—no—and swipe my hand across the slick beads.

"It's okay," Gigi says. I drop my hand to my side and look over my shoulder at Gigi sitting between my parents, hunched over, a head shorter than them. "Go ahead, you can touch it. My pipe is inside there."

I carefully pick up each piece of fringe, one by one, let them slide between my middle finger and thumb, and place my whole hand on the bag—pipe inside like a bone.

"Try holding your palm over the bag. Almost touching but not."

I lift my hand a little.

"Feel anything?" she asks.

"Like what?" I ask, glancing back. Mom has a wary look on her face, but Gigi can't see it.

Damon gets up from the sofa to take our plates to the kitchen. He tries to take Naima's, but she stops him. "I'm not finished," she says, mouth full of chicken.

"Anything inside your palm," Gigi says.

*She can't be talking about my insides*, I think, and say, "Umm."

"Close your eyes and try to feel inside your palm."

*She really is talking about my insides.* Sweet relief swims through my cells like I've just confessed a secret, and I close my eyes and feel tiny dots, tingles, in the middle of my palm. Heat—a soft heat, not the kind that burns, the kind I feel every time I press my palms together in prayer—travels from the middle of my hand to the tips of my fingers. I want to tell Gigi everything: my doubts about good people going to hell just because they happen to be a different religion or happen to mow their lawns or wash their cars or plant begonias on

Sunday instead of going to church. Most of all, I want to tell Gigi about the God I feel inside me when I get still. I want to know if that God is the same God we learn about in church, but something about Gigi sitting between my parents makes my tongue curl up tight in my mouth, won't let me mix my insides with my out.

"It's okay. You can stop. I was trying to let you feel the energy of your ancestors. That's all," Gigi says.

I open my eyes, but I can't turn around, can't look at Mom's face. "From heaven?" I ask, staring at the turquoise stars.

"Wherever they are."

"From hell?"

"Wherever they are."

"I wanna try!" Naima says, jumping up. "Ouch!" She rubs the back of her thighs where the plastic on the sofa yanked her skin like a Band-Aid.

"Sit down," Mom says. She stands up and starts clearing the table. I think Gigi's words have turned too far from what we learn in our pews at church.

"The bag and the pipe belonged to my father, his father, and his father, a Cherokee Freedman," Gigi continues, over the clank of forks and plates in the kitchen.

"A real Indian?" I ask.

"I got Indian in my family," girls at school always brag. People only believe the ones with good hair. People call the ones with kinky hair liars. When my hair gets nappy, I get it pressed. But Mom says when I turn thirteen I can get a perm. I want to have straight hair forever, like Gigi. Even though it's silver, it's silky smooth.

"Yes, a slave and son of a Cherokee," Gigi says. "Picked cotton. Set free. Built a school for Red-Black Cherokee up near Double Springs Creek." Gigi's words come slow, as if she has to pluck each one from a part of her mind that has already traveled somewhere high in the sky. I wait for each word to fall on my ears like I wait for stray raindrops to fall on my skin on days with gray skies.

"So that would make him my great-great-great-great-grandfather?"

"Yes," Gigi says, standing up. She slowly starts to make her way toward me. Each time she brings one foot up to meet the next, I'm afraid her rounded back will tip her over. I see a silver cane leaning against the TV, but I'm too afraid to touch it. I think about meeting her and giving her my arm for support, but I'm too afraid of her touching me. So, I just stand there and wait.

"That's . . . a . . . lot . . . of . . . greats," I say, as slow as her steps, praying each word will magically hold her up.

"Yes. And your great-great-grandmother is in this picture doing my hair. My mother. Me," she says, pointing. "And me again with my husband. You never met him . . . he died when you were just a baby."

*You're the beautiful woman with high cheeks?* I think, and look down at her blue, watery eyes. The folds of skin in her sunken face. The thinning strip of hair traveling down the middle of her silver head. Her tiny bones tightly wrapped with skin so thin, I can see every dark blotch and dot beneath its surface. *How could this beautiful woman and pretty little girl be you? If they look like you now, what would I look like at your age? I'm not even that pretty to begin with.* I start to feel hot and nauseous all over again. I can't stand beside this many greats anymore. I go back to sit down between Naima and Damon, where I'm comfortable, not daring to budge until we leave.

Daddy's car phone rings soon after we cross the Texas border. Mom opens the center console and hands the phone to Daddy. "Hello," he answers.

"I see," he says, his voice cracking. Daddy slows down and pulls over on the side of the dark highway.

"Okay, I'll be back in the morning." He hangs up.

"She's gone," he says to Mom.

"I'm so sorry, Jim," Mom says.

With her long chin meeting her left shoulder, she looks into the backseat. I pretend to be asleep along with Naima and Damon so she won't have to search for words. Then she leans over and hugs Daddy.

Warm tears roll down both of my cheeks, but I don't wipe them.

Mom lets go of Daddy and asks, "Do we need to head back?"

"No, I'll fly back in the morning. You and the kids can come this weekend."

"Okay, I'll drive the rest of the way."

They get out and exchange seats.

In the dark silence of the car ride home, I wonder where Gigi's soul has gone. I think about heaven and hell, but remember what she told me, *Wherever they are.* Her words are strangely mixing into the silence of the car, into the news of her death, and into my questions about God. With my insides tingling, I can feel her. I pray she can feel me, too. I pray she can feel that I was afraid, know that I am sorry for being afraid, and forgive me.

# Turquoise Sky

One by one, they walk down the red-carpeted aisle of the sanctuary. White robes waving like flags of peace. White head scarves of modesty. No high heels, big hats, or makeup. Only wholesome faces holding the slight smile of the Mona Lisa.

*What are nuns doing here?* I write on the cover of the church bulletin underneath large red letters that spell *welcome* and angle the note toward Keisha, sitting on my right. I slip my left hand into the aisle to feel the passing of the white robes—soft cotton waves lapping my fingertips.

*Not nuns. MUSLIMS*, she writes back, and looks at me, widening the white of her upturned eyes.

I pull my hand out of the aisle and place it in my lap. The only Muslims I've been this close to are the boys that wear bow ties while selling newspapers and bean pies on the corners of West Montgomery Road in Acres Homes. We ride through Acres Homes every Sunday and Wednesday to go to church, every Saturday in the summer to go to the library to return and pick out books. At red lights, I get close enough to touch the Muslims, but glass always separates us. Mom makes us ride through Acres Homes with our windows up.

A solitary man ends the line. No bow tie. Looks straight ahead. Walks as perfectly upright as his round, white hat— shaped like a flat top. Has a full beard, like Pastor Hayes.

In front of me, Sister Hyde shifts her obese body from side to side, looking uncomfortable with the aisle seat of the ninth pew she claims every Sunday. The purple feathers sticking out of the side of her purple hat flap up and down like they want to fly away. Across the aisle from me, Sister Hobbs turns the pages of her Bible faster than she can possibly read, while Sister Booker, sitting behind her, rapidly fans her face, her narrow eyes staring straight into the empty pulpit, or maybe beyond the pulpit to the front wall, where a painted Jesus descends from the clouds.

One by one, the people in white sit down in the front pew, to Pastor Hayes's left, in front of Mom and the other deaconesses, who moved back a pew for their guests, across the aisle from the deacons, where Daddy sits.

*Why are they here?* I write.

Keisha scribbles a question mark, but after turning to exchange long whispers with Mona at her other side, leans in toward me, and whispers, "They're from California."

I picture the earth splitting underneath a steady turquoise sky.

"They came to Houston for a women's conference and invited the deaconesses because Sister Langley's daughter goes to their mosque—you know, the one Sister Langley is always asking the church to pray for, asking Jesus to save. Anyways, the deaconesses didn't go, but to be polite, they returned an invitation to our church. And they actually came," she says.

I want to know if Sister Langley's daughter is here. She might be able to tell me the secret for thinking a different way without being afraid of going to hell. But I just say, "Oh," because I can't take any more of Keisha's hot breath in my ear and on my neck.

After the children's choir sings, the little ones exit the choir stand behind Pastor Hayes and file out the side door of the sanctuary to the trailer for children's church. Everyone gives them a standing ovation as they leave—heads nodding, *amen*s flying, hands clapping, the sleeves of their white robes flapping like wings.

"Yes, Lord!" Pastor Hayes says loudly into the pulpit microphone. "Give those children another round of applause." He claps with black wings, robe draped with bars bearing scarlet crosses. Pastor Hayes stops clapping and puts on his serious face. "Who is Jesus?"

As soon as I hear the first words of Pastor Hayes's sermon, I know exactly which one it is—the unless-you're-saved-you're-going-to-hell sermon. He preaches it at least ten times a year. Shuffling the words like cards in a deck. Doesn't matter how he cuts them. I know them. Can't shake them. His words ride the waves of questions and doubts that visit me in bed at night. I pray the waves away, shaking with the fear they mean I'm not saved. Fear that if I die in my sleep, God won't hear my prayers and I will ride my waves straight to hell.

I look down at Keisha's sermon notes. She's already on her third bullet point: *You can either choose Jesus as your Lord and savior or as your . . .*

"You can either choose Jesus as your Lord and savior or as your judge!" Pastor Hayes shouts. He always repeats the important points, the bullet points, to make sure they sink in. Bullet point one: *Jesus is the Son of God*. Bullet point two: *Jesus is the only way to God*.

Nothing but white space lies between the lines on the back of my bulletin. I look ahead at the white robes. They are still, attentive, polite. I picture their white wings flapping, flying over Jesus's head into the painted white clouds. God hearing their prayers and opening the turquoise sky.

# Black-Infested

*The black people are coming! The black people are coming! Look. Run. Hide. They're on their way. Right here to Inwood. Right here to your street. They're coming. Soon you could be surrounded on all four sides. One side was bad enough, but all four sides? They're coming. Run, Reina, run. Run, Pam, run. Run, Becky, run. What are you still doing here, Theresa? Run.*

That's what I swear I can hear blaring from the speakers of the ice cream truck we pass turning into our neighborhood.

"Who would eat ice cream right now? So stupid," I say, looking out the window—no December sun. This year it's gray and cold.

"I would!" Naima says. "Mom, can I—"

"No," Mom says. She's not happy about all the For Sale signs either.

Now that one too many black people have moved into Inwood, For Sale signs are everywhere, and the whole kickball crew is gone. Pam and I were starting to get close. She'd even invited me to stand with her circle of friends at school a few times.

Naima wasn't close with Becky or Theresa, but she still misses playing kickball.

Damon doesn't care. His friend got a new speaker for the trunk of his car and they bump their music louder down the block.

If Daddy cares, there are no signs or words to tell.

"Eight signs," I say, riding in the passenger seat, counting For Sale signs as we drive down our street.

"Nope, nine," Naima says, from the backseat. I forgot to count Pam's. I don't like looking at their yard anymore. The leaves of their red begonias have passed from yellow to brown to none.

"If we could afford to move, we'd be gone, too," Mom says, turning in to our driveway. "At least we live in Inwood North instead of Inwood Pines, the side closest to Acres Homes, where all of them are coming from."

# Gold Hoops

I look myself over in the mirror. Big forehead, long chin—nothing I can do about that. I look at the outlines of my bra, showing through my white T-shirt. No one even cares about bras and boobs anymore; it's all about big butts. My ponytail isn't high enough. No, it's on the wrong side. I take off my tangerine scrunchie, grip my hair, brush it up and over to the far left, lifting my hand out of the way with each stroke, and wrap the cloth-covered elastic band around my tightfisted hair until it has no more to give.

A high ponytail to the right is usually my favorite hairstyle, but all morning it seems to be giggling under its breath. I'm about to say forget the left side, too, take my ponytail down for good when I hear Mom's muffled voice through the bathroom door say, "Taja, you better hurry up and get outside! The bus will be here in seven minutes!"

The ponytail stays and I settle on bringing out my baby hair. I hate baby hair. It looks stupid on anyone old enough to ride a bike without training wheels. But all the new girls wear their baby hair in big waves, so I brush the tiniest bit of hair away from my hairline—boar bristles scratching my face—shape the hair into small waves, and add gel to keep them in place.

I hold my head to one side, then the other, smile with my lips pressed together, put my left hand on my left hip, take it off, try my right hand on my right hip. Something is off about my outfit: a white V-neck T-shirt tied in a knot at my right hip and tangerine shorts. I untie the knot. Tie it on my left hip. The right hip is better. I wish I'd left it alone. I untie the knot again. Tie it one more time on the right.

"Taja, you better bring your butt out here! I'm not driving you to school!" Mom yells.

She doesn't realize I'm about to be put to the test, the same test I've taken every day since the first day of school. The first test I don't know how to study for, don't know how to ace. Each time I pass this new girl, LaToya, and her friends on the bus going to school, in the auditorium before the first bell, in the halls between every class, in the cafeteria holding my tray trying to find a table to sit at with Amber—a girl in all my honors classes whose family stayed—I hear them say:

She ain't nothing but a wannabe white girl.

She must think she white.

She's just a black *white* girl. Can't help herself.

That's it! She's Black White Girl.

Black White Girl, I can fit a jump rope between your two front teeth.

Black White Girl, you got the Jolly Green Giant beat.

Black White Girl, how'd you get so tall?

Black White Girl, them boats on your ankles about to make you trip and fall.

I always pretend not to hear. What else am I supposed to do? Say something and get beat down? I don't think so.

I roll my neck at myself in the bathroom mirror with twisted lips to see how I would look if I got bold enough to tell somebody off. I stop twisting my lips. Rolling my long neck was enough, especially with my new gold earrings. I love my huge hoops, same ones the new girls wear. The saleswoman told me I could wear them as bangles, too, but I never do. I want to feel them bouncing against my cheeks all day, dangling free. Plus, if I ever lower my head too much, they touch my collarbones and remind me to look up.

"Taja!" Mom yells, and bangs on the door.

I open it. Rush out. Make it in time. The bus stops right in front of our house and takes me from day to day, week to week, and month to month of the same girls saying the same things. But at the end of March, as I stand on the stage, accepting my award for receiving 100 percent in every class, for the whole month, I catch a glimpse of myself in the certificate's shiny gold stamp and finger my baby hair back, away from my face. I know I'm not going to get stuck on the bus with those girls. I'm going to travel to places too far for them to see, miles and miles outside of being *black*, past the snap of their fingers with the complementary "Baby, boom," "Baby, pop," or "Baby, please," past anything they say about me until I can feel them so far behind that I can look back and see stupid little girls, still occasionally talking their smack, pushing me on.

# A Dirty Secret

"Ewwww, Taja has boo-boo on her pants," Naima says.

"Shut up," I say, bent over, face in the fridge, looking for something cool to drink. No Tang, no lemonade. No Kool-Aid either, but that's nothing new; Kool-Aid stains, and Mom can't stand stains on her carpet.

I look over to the sink: plastic pitcher empty. "Now somebody's dead wrong," I say. The rule is: whoever drinks the last glass makes the next batch. Clearly, somebody didn't follow the rule. I bet it was Naima. I stand up straight, turn around, and roll my eyes at Naima, who's sitting with Damon at the kitchen counter, already eating her tuna sandwich—Tuesday's afternoon snack.

I walk past Mom at the stove; she's holding a book and stirring something in a pot. Reading and cooking. Smells like gumbo. Gumbo and *Cane*. Yesterday it was meat loaf and *Cane*. The day before that, salmon cakes and *Cane*. I stand on my tiptoes and grab the Tang from the top shelf.

Damon laughs and says, "You really do have something on your butt." His laugh shoots high and then punches the air without a sound.

I twist myself to check out what he's laughing at, but I don't see anything on my orange track shorts. I recently made the team. Placed first in the long, triple, and high jumps at the first two meets. Coach June says I'm one of the best middle-school jumpers she's ever seen. Says my long legs may even be able to pay for college.

"And . . . and," he says, eyes watering, shoulders bouncing, "from here, it looks a lot like boo-boo."

"Told you," Naima says, and licks a bit of tuna off her bottom lip.

Mom puts her book down, grabs my shoulders, and turns me around. "That's enough from you two," she says, and leads me by the hand into her room. Naima tries to follow, but Mom gives her a firm "Go sit down." She closes the door behind us.

Did I really boo-boo on myself? How did I not feel it

coming out? It must have been the sneaky kind, the sick kind. But I'm not sick. I'm in deep trouble. I can already hear Mom, *You're too old for this, Taja*, like she says if she ever catches me musty. But musty doesn't have a thing on this. *Trouble* is not even the word for what I'm in. But the way Mom guides me through her sitting room past her waterbed doesn't feel like trouble. Feels like something else, something soft like . . . I don't know. It's the way she's holding my hand, her limp fingers laced with mine, delicate like . . . like sympathy.

When we get to the bathroom, I quickly turn to look at my butt in the mirror. No! How could it be? How did a nasty brown stain get on my track shorts?

"It's not what you think," Mom says, but I still start to cry. "I'm so sorry. This is my fault. You should have been better prepared." She hugs me close, her big breasts pressing into my ribs, and talks about how my body is changing, how when girls get a certain age, their uterus, ovaries, and fallopian tubes start preparing to make babies. Fallopian tubes sound strange, and I picture a tiny baby coming headfirst out of a tube of toothpaste, and stop crying.

Mom releases her hug and says, "Right?"

"Huh?" I say, looking down at the top of her head.

She turns, looks at me in the mirror, and says, "But you won't have a baby for a long time, right?"

I look at her in the mirror and say, "Right."

"Until after you finish college and get married, right?" Her eyes are locked with mine.

*College*. Coach June says I could go as far away as California. *California*, and I picture a bright turquoise sky.

"Right, Taja?"

"Right, Mom."

"Do you remember our talk about sex after the girl at your school got pregnant?"

"Yeah, Mom," I say, and look away, tired of the question game, trying to think of the girl's name—Asha, no, Aisha. I remember her walking toward me down the hall, holding one end of her headphones to the front of her sweatshirt and the other to her ear, while silently singing along. I tried to read her lips to see if I knew the song, but something about the way her lips floated open, the way her eyelids lingered each time they closed, made me feel wrong for watching, like I was eavesdropping, so I looked away. The next day, in halls humming *Aisha's pregnant*, she walked with no headphones, head hung low. The day after that, she was gone.

"Right?" Mom says.

I can feel her eyes widening at me in the mirror. "Huh?"

"Because you know sex before marriage is a sin, right?"

"Right, Mom!"

◆ ◆ ◆

A month later, my period comes while I'm at school. Now instead of getting to English early, turning my notebook to a clean page, and writing the date in the upper right-hand corner, I'm in a bathroom stall, staring at a dark, ragged heart, bleeding on both sides of the seam in my jeans. I rub it with a fistful of toilet paper, wet with my spit, and pray for God to wash it away like a sin, but it won't come clean. I refuse to look at it anymore. I toss the wad in the bowl between my parted legs and gaze at the love-hate notes on the back of the blue door, waiting for the last two girls to leave so they won't hear me put on a pad.

I hear a toilet flush, a metal lock click, and quick, squeaky steps away from me. The roar from the hall rushes in, and out goes a girl without washing her hands—nasty, but I'm happy she's gone. Only one more left; she's in the stall next to me.

The three-minute bell rings. I start opening the white plastic wrapper slowly, groove by groove, to minimize the sound, wishing I had the kind the TV commercial promises opens discreetly. This is taking way too long, so I close my eyes, take a deep breath, and brace myself for the loud zipper-like sound of the wrapper. Before I pull, I hear plastic ripping apart, paper peeling and crumpling, and stainless steel hitting stainless steel as the trash bin's lid slams down.

*You, too!* I put on my pad, quickly and freely, and pull up my pants, shirt on the outside to cover the brown spot. The wrinkles on the bottom of my shirt look stupid, but I'll take bad fashion over a stain that looks like boo-boo.

As I walk toward the sink, the girl pushes white foam out of the soap dispenser and turns on the water. I smile at the wrinkles on the bottom of her shirt and look at her muted blue eyes in the mirror, waiting to exchange understanding glances. But she won't look at me. She lowers her head until her pale blond hair slides over her face. We wash our hands, light-red-stained water splattering onto the sides of white sinks that we quickly rinse out. Then without pushing the big silver button for hot air, we rush toward the bright blue door. She holds it open for me—her wet hand pressing into the bell-skirted silhouette, her long hair still hiding her face.

"Thanks," I say, accepting the weight of the door, and she takes off running down the hall.

The tardy bell rings, but I'm still here, staring at the symbol for women, wondering why we're the ones who have to make babies, why we're the ones who have to deal with the blood, the stains, the shame.

# Deep Dimples

I've already given up bacon, butter-pecan ice cream, and new books, but a present for my birthday? Am I supposed to give that up, too? Mom says money is tight right now. Daddy keeps on as normal. Every day he puts on a suit and tie and carries his briefcase out the door, like normal. He comes home, gives hugs and kisses, and smiles with deep dimples, like normal. But Mom makes sure we know things aren't normal, says we're old enough to learn what it means to sacrifice.

But Daddy already promised me my bracelet: thick, chain-linked silver with a dangling butterfly. Costs $69.99. My initials can be engraved on the butterfly's wings to make it my own, make it special, but that would be an extra $9.99, and I don't want to be greedy. I can sacrifice my initials until Daddy finds a new job.

He had a job selling insurance when I saw the bracelet in the store, where we found Mom's Mother's Day gift—a thin gold necklace with a ruby-red heart.

"Oh, pretty!" I said, looking into the glass case near the cash register.

"You like that?" Daddy said.

"Love it!"

"Tell you what, we'll come back and get it for your birthday."

"Promise?"

"Promise."

Before we left the store, the lady behind the counter gave us her card—a white rectangle with raised purple letters, *Mary Turner* in cursive, now calling me from the bottom corner of my dresser mirror, where I tucked the card two months ago.

With only three days until my birthday, it's time to talk to Mary Turner. Can't use the phone in the kitchen, because Mom is cooking. So I use Damon's phone to make sure my bracelet is still there. "It is indeed," Mary Turner says, "pretty as ever." She remembers me. I am pretty, too. My bracelet is waiting for me, the last one, so I better not make it wait too long.

After I hang up, I slip the card into the back pocket of my Guess jeans and try to get Daddy alone. Doesn't happen before dinner: rice and pinto beans.

"The beans are good, Bev," Daddy says.

"Yeah, Mom, real good," Damon adds.

Then even Naima says, "Yeah, Mommy," and licks the bean juice off her bottom lip.

I don't say anything. I hate Wednesday's pinto beans. Tuesday's black-eyed peas aren't bad. I can even take the rest of the week's black, baked, red, kidney, and garbanzo beans. But pinto beans are the worst. I'm tired of beans. After a month and a half, I know we've eaten more than enough of them to save $69.99. I can't wait until Saturday when I get a break from beans. For my birthday, Mom promised me ice cream and pizza. What's a slumber party without ice cream and pizza? Beans and slumber party don't even match.

After dinner Daddy sits in his black leather recliner, in the corner by the window, and draws circles in the newspaper. I lie on the sofa beside his chair and pretend to read *The Dream Keeper*, by Langston Hughes. It's easy to pretend because I've already read it three times. Mom walks in from the dining room, bowl and drying towel in hand, and says, "Taja, come on out of there and give your daddy some space."

"It's okay," Daddy says.

Mom turns, eyes me over her left shoulder, and walks away.

I allow a few minutes to pass, turn a few pages, and then say, "Saturday's my birthday!" packing extra excitement into each syllable.

"I know. My little girl is growing up." Daddy makes another circle in the paper. "Excited about your slumber party?"

"Yes." But he didn't ask me what I want for my birthday. Daddy always asks me what I want. Bringing up the bracelet would be easier if he asked, but it's going to be hard. "You know the store where we found Mom's Mother's Day gift?" I say, staring at a blur of small, black words in my book.

"Sure, I remember."

"Remember what you promised?" *Promised*. As soon as I say that word, I feel guilt sink into my chest like a weight on the end of a fishing line just cast into the sea. But I want my bracelet, so I reel it in. Wait for an answer.

"Oh, yeah, how could . . . could I forget your bracelet?" he says, and clears his throat.

A weight must be caught at the top of his throat like it's at the top of mine. It won't let me breathe, won't let me speak another word. So I swallow it, feel it hit the bottom of my stomach, and settle. I gasp for air and say, "So I can get it?"

A pause. A smile with no deep dimples. "Of course you can," he says, straining to sound happy, normal. "Anything for your birthday. We'll go early Saturday morning to pick it up."

I jump up and say, "Thank you, Daddy!" Kiss his cheek—rough with stubble and wet with sweat—and take off running as fast as I can down the hall, away from the pit I left Daddy sinking in, in the corner of the room.

*But the truth has a strange way of following you,*

*of coming up to you and making you*

*listen to what it has to say.*

—Sandra Cisneros, "One Holy Night"

# Chocolate Mourning

**D**addy gets up when it's still dark, when he thinks nobody's awake, and holds a saxophone he cannot play. He keeps the saxophone in a black case in the closet under the stairs. On the outside the case looks like the one he used to take to work each day, only bigger.

He sits with the case on his lap in his favorite chair, in the corner by the window. The window is open and crickets sing in the chocolate darkness, a choir of a million.

He wedges his thumbs underneath two golden latches on either side of the handle. The backs of his thumbs rub against his big, soft belly—still my favorite place to lay my head. The latches click and the top of the case pops up, but only slightly. He raises the top until the golden latches face the sky. His face looks as happy as the saxophone's yellow brass. He runs his fingers over the purple velvet inside. I wish I could feel what he's feeling.

I move up from Naima's and my doorway to Damon's doorway. Damon's door is closed, so I crouch down in the hallway's darkness. This is where I usually stay so the soft, yellow light from Daddy's lamp won't catch my face.

He slips the black strap over his head and around his neck. He screws the mouthpiece into a small brass piece shaped like his tobacco pipe on the table by the lamp. A wavy stream of smoke floats out the window. Smells like the chocolate-flavored kind—my favorite. Smells like the butter toffee Mom makes in the skillet—so sweet. Mom doesn't allow smoking in the house, so I only smell the sweetness of Daddy's tobacco on car rides and early mornings like these.

He connects the brass pipe to the saxophone and lifts it from its case. He puts the mouthpiece to his lips and fills his cheeks with breath until they look pregnant. But he doesn't blow out. He never blows out. I've never heard the saxophone make a sound. "Blow, Daddy, blow," I mouth. But he can't see my lips moving in the darkness.

I crawl closer, from Damon's doorway to the doorway Daddy shares with Mom. Yellow light catches my yellow arm, and I lie down in the darkness. Carpet itches my long, bare legs, and I scratch them until it hurts. His cheeks are still pregnant. They must hurt. His lungs must hurt. He's never held his breath this long.

Closer, I see his eyes are closed. Closer, I see his face isn't shining like the brass he holds. Besides his cheeks, his face is soft in a way I've never seen, like ice cream that sat in a bowl too long and is starting to melt away.

He fingers the brass keys but doesn't press down. I close my eyes to listen to his silent song. I never knew these mornings sounded so sad, like the lost notes of a sweet dream. He stops fingering, removes his lips from the saxophone, and lets out his breath.

I want to go to him, lay my head on his big belly, and say, "Daddy, everything will be okay." I want to say, "It's not too late to learn how to play." I want to tell him, "I'm so sorry for making you take four bills from your worn wallet, twenty by twenty, and lay them on Mary Turner's counter." But I can't. I'm too afraid of his sadness.

I slide away from him, returning to bed. I don't want to feel what he's feeling. I don't want to wake up before the sun and pretend to play something I've never learned to play. I don't want cheeks pregnant with chocolate smoke—lost dreams packed away in a black case.

# About Time

In the dizzy heat of September, in the noon sun that knocks at our closed window and falls away in waves, in that blurriness, I see a strong, brown arm, hammering in the backyard. Then I see Daddy.

He must feel me staring at him through our bedroom window because he turns and says, "Is this too loud?" His words lose strength crossing through the glass, but I make them out, shake my head, and he turns his focus back to building our tall cedar fence.

He's been putting up fences ever since Ms. Stevens's house got robbed. They took her TV, VCR, microwave, and dog—"Everything I loved," she told the police. And that's how Daddy got his new job.

Everyone wants new fences, higher than before, and Daddy knows how to build them. He started with simple designs: side by side or board on board. But weeks later, when the police arrested three teenage girls who came from nice homes and explained they were bored, people sighed, said, "White people are crazy," and asked for more: trelliswork, arched walkways, decks, and rooms without walls. Mom wants to stay on the safe side, stick with a new fence—simple, tall.

Outside my window, Daddy looks strange without his big belly. His sweaty, white T-shirt clings to soft, sagging rolls—no longer a good place to lay my head. But it's about time for me to stop that anyway. I'm getting older. He looks younger, with muscles and slim cheeks, like a different man. "A new man," everybody tells him, and pats him on the back. He always laughs and says, "That's what swinging a hammer in that Houston heat will do to you."

Nobody messes with that Houston heat. That Houston heat does not play. It kills people, young and old, running on fields, lying in hospital beds and cribs in non-air-conditioned homes.

I can only see Daddy from one side, but I can still tell he isn't worried about the heat. He doesn't wipe sweat; he doesn't fan himself; he lets whatever the heat burns slide right off his left temple, down the side of his face, off his chin, and wet his neck, chest, and belly. Daddy's elbow even drips with sweat. His silver watch drips with sweat. It hangs away from his left wrist and slides down his hand with each swing of the hammer. Just looking at it rush back and forth annoys me. It must have been bothering him, too, because he finally takes it off, places it in the grass, and goes back to swinging.

Daddy has it figured out. How to lose his thoughts somewhere in swinging, in hitting hammer to nail, and leave them where metal meets metal, where time is still, right there in the silver scratches on the head. It's the timing of his movements, of their sounds, that give it all away. Once thoughts are gone, rhythm shows up like clear skin on picture day. Oh, the grace, the music: a series of knocks and ensuing rings, metal meeting metal meeting wood, and passing through our bedroom window, strength not lost, passed on—ringing in yellow waves. I listen while reading at my desk underneath the window, and imitate the music by tapping my pencil and metal pen against the metal legs of my chair—same beat, similar sounds. I switch it up, listen— similar beat, different sounds. I switch it up, listen—different beat, different sounds. I listen.

# Waves

**D**amon is getting ready for a date. He dips his finger into a small orange can of Murray's pomade that promises waves. The pomade is thick, like the bacon grease in the glass jar by the stove. He rubs the pomade between his hands like a homeless man in front of a burning garbage can in the cold. He strokes the pomade on his low-cut fade and brushes his hair—crown to forehead, crown to temples, crown to ears, crown to neck—to bring out the waves.

"You know you see these waves," he says, cocking his head to the side for me to see. I'm sitting on his bed, flipping through a *Jet* magazine. He buys them just to get the Beauty of the Week. They're all torn out and pinned up on the wall behind me. I wish I could save them—take them down, cut them out, and put proper clothes on them like they were my old paper dolls—but Damon would kill me.

"What waves?" I squint playfully. How could I miss the deep grooves in his hair? He works on them night and day. Wave caps, do-rags, brushes, pomade, and Rogaine. Eleventh grade and already the hair at his temples is starting to thin. It's hereditary. He's fighting it, though, like Bruce Lee over there in the corner, inside the thirteen-inch TV.

"You know these waves are about to get you seasick in here," he says, and laughs with no sound. Broad shoulders bounce, perfect teeth shine, glossy tears in his big, black eyes.

"Whatever."

His phone rings (he has his own line). Mom said she wasn't about to be a secretary half the day and at home all night. It rings again. "Answer it," he says, holding out his greasy hands.

"Hello."

There's music playing on the other end. Oh, wait. It's Tony! Toni! Toné! I like this song. "'It's our anniversary, made for you and me,'" I sing along. When I spend the night at Keisha's house, we make calls like these to cute boys. Fun for now, but at Damon's age, I hope we'll have better things to do with ourselves.

I've had enough, am about to hang up, when a girl says, "Hello."

"Hello."

The music lowers.

"Hello," I repeat.

The girl hangs up.

"It looks like you have a secret admirer," I tell Damon. He's lacing up his Jordans, the red ones, his favorite pair. Maybe we'll finally get to meet a girl. Haven't found any *worthy* to bring home yet, he's always explaining to Mom; *the good ones are rare*.

"Well, what can I say," Damon says, stroking his invisible mustache, "your boy has a lot of admirers."

"Boy, please!" I roll my eyes as hard as I can. My eyelashes flutter. I can only see waves of light. Is this what it's like to be blind? It hurts. I stop.

That evening, over fried catfish, corn cakes, and Daddy's latest building project, Damon's phone rings again. And again and again. Mom gets up to close Damon's door. Daddy plays Coltrane on the stereo. Naima isn't here to complain; she's at a friend's.

That night, as I pray for thicker legs, a bigger booty, and my first kiss, Damon's phone rings again. I stop praying. Amen.

As I stumble into Damon's room, the smell of feet and Fritos smacks me in the nose. It always stinks in here, but it's worse because the door has been closed. I head for the nightstand and feel for the phone.

"Hello."

Whitney Houston is singing one of my favorite songs, "I Will Always Love You," but I'm too tired to sing along.

"Hello," I say louder, angrier.

"Hello." Same girl as earlier, but sounds like she caught a cold.

"Damon isn't here."

"Is this Taja?"

"Taja. How do you know my name?"

"Damon always talks about you." She makes her words sound sweet, like my aunts do when they call from out of state.

I feel for the lamp on the nightstand and switch on the light, soft as a full moon over the Gulf of Mexico.

"I'm Tanisha." She speaks her name with confidence, like I should know it. "Damon's ex-girlfriend."

Ex-*girlfriend*? Damon's never said he's had a girlfriend. Only girls. I'm about to ask her if she's sure her terminology is correct, when she begins to cry. "Please don't cry." She cries louder. "Please. Everything will be okay." She quiets down for a second, and then cries out again. Her heartache rises and falls inside me. I want to save her. "Please stop. It will be okay. I'm sure y'all will work it out. I'll tell Damon to call you in the morning. Okay?"

"No. Wait. Please don't hang up."

I look at the alarm clock on the nightstand. Two strokes to midnight.

"I heard you singing earlier. Your voice has a nice tone." She's stopped crying.

"Thanks."

"Are you part of the school choir?" Her sweet voice is back.

"No, but I sing in the teen choir at church."

"I bet you get a lot of solos."

"No, I don't."

"Why not? You should."

"The pastor's daughters get all the solos—duets, too. They're twins, you see, Mona and Brandy. The congregation gives them a standing ovation every time they sing. Now, you know that doesn't make sense. Every time? They can't even sing if you ask me."

"Well, it sounds like Mona and Brandy need to stop hogging all the solos and give them to somebody who can really sing." I like the way she says Mona's and Brandy's names, like they stink.

I laugh and climb on top of the bed—a mattress sitting on a tall wooden box covered with dark blue carpet. Damon built it with Daddy.

"You're really nice," Tanisha says. "I can tell we'd have fun listening to CDs and painting each other's nails. I wear mine pink, hot pink." When she says, "hot pink," her voice goes from sweet to . . . something else. Like it could belong to one of the girls on Damon's wall.

She keeps talking, as if she knows me, as if she's my friend, especially when she describes how they first kissed. I can't listen to all the details. Damon *is* my brother. But I let her talk.

The *Jet* is still on his bed. It's opened to the Beauty of the Week. He hasn't torn her out yet. She's not really a beauty, just has a big booty. Big hair, a red bikini, and makeup help, but not enough. I close her against the Murray's pomade ad on the opposite page and place her inside the Bible, on the nightstand, where she can rest before being ripped out and tacked up.

I tune back in. Their first fight. "He acted like he didn't even know me. He knew he saw me waiting by the trophy case after his baseball game. I said 'Hey,' plain as day, and he looked straight at me and kept walking." They made up the next day. Second base. Time to tune out again.

Damon has a real Bible, not the teenage edition. His name is engraved on the front. I trace the gold-leaf letters with my fingers. My fingernails are bare, and I imagine them painted hot pink. I take the Bible from the nightstand and put it in my lap, fingers stiff, careful, like my nails are wet.

I open to a page bleeding with dark blue ink. Crossed-out words with *hair* written in their place. I read 1 Corinthians, chapter three, verse seven, "So then neither the one who plants nor the one who waters is anything, but God who causes *hair* growth." I didn't know Damon's hair waded this deep. Deep blue splashes over my knees. I want to run, but something inside me makes me turn to another chapter. More blue ink. Proverbs twenty-seven, twenty-five, "When the *hair* disappears, the new *hair* growth is seen . . . "

Deep blue swells over my head. I can't stop myself from feeling Damon's pain, can't stop myself from crying. Tanisha is crying, too.

"I knew you would feel me," she says. "I just want to be with him."

She doesn't even know my brother. Hasn't dipped a toe in his pain. "We all want things we can't have, don't we?" I shouldn't have even told this girl my name.

"What? Why are you being like this? I thought we were friends. You and your brother can sure flip the switch—"

"I'm sorry," I say, and I hang up. Forget painting my nails hot pink. I open the *Jet* magazine. Beauty of the Week stares right at me, stares at anybody who wants to see. Damon loves to see. Maybe that's the beauty's pride. Maybe attention is what all his girls need. Maybe that's what Tanisha cries for. *Why did I hang up?* That was mean, probably made her cry even more. But Damon hurts, too. And maybe her needs are what it takes to keep his head above the deep blue.

# God Don't
# Like Ugly

For a year and a half, I've been praying to be kissed. You know, really kissed. Not like that weak, sloppy kiss George gave to Brandy. Like that *Boyz n the Hood* kiss when Ricky and his girlfriend are at the barbecue, and he smooth-walks up to her and steals her mouth, first with his lips, then with his sweet tongue. You know it's sweet. And his lips grab hers, his tongue rolls, licks, sucks.

Yeah, that kind of kiss.

I'm tired of lying about Terrance kissing me last year. He's from Atlanta, so it's an easy lie. I sure did want to kiss him when him and his parents (college friends of my parents) stopped to spend the night on their drive down to Corpus Christi. I especially wanted to kiss him as I lay between him and Naima on the living room floor (his parents took Naima's and my bedroom). His lips looked so sweet when he was asleep. They didn't burp, spit, or say mean things when he was asleep. But kissing Terrance wasn't in God's plan for me. He probably would've tried something extra, anyway, and I'm not fast like that.

Now we're on Christmas vacation with our church at the National Baptist Convention in Detroit. There are plenty of boys here and plenty of opportunities to get my kiss, not to mention plenty of finger waves, Jheri curls, gator shoes, and pimp suits. Let me stop—God don't like ugly. All day the grown-ups are on the other side of the convention center, probably learning about the Bible and how to be better Christians, like we do every Sunday. And the preteens and teens have the option of choir or theater. Damon said he chose choir because, "That's where all the fine girls are." Naima and her friends chose choir, too.

I chose theater and now I'm in the auditorium practicing a big play we'll perform for our parents on the last day. Keisha, Brandy, Mona, and I don't have lines. We just throw stones and get stoned, not like they did in *Friday*, but like they tried to do in the Book of John when the Pharisees caught that woman cheating on her husband. Jesus stopped them, though.

Keisha knows no one has kissed me. I don't have to lie to

her. She doesn't make fun of me. She only got her first kiss this year. We're slow together. Now *slow* is not the word for Mona and Brandy. They've kissed so many boys. And I know they're not lying, because I've seen them with my own two eyes: behind the church, in the Sunday school room, in the nursery, sometimes right before their daddy preaches, sometimes with the same boy, one twin right after the other. Now that's nasty. But I'm not the one to throw stones. That's only my part in the play.

Me, Keisha, and this boy named Dorian throw paper stones at Mona and Brandy because they get pregnant. It's weird because their older sister, Ayana, really did get pregnant last year. Sixteen. Had the baby. And I swear, if eyes could throw stones, then there would be piles of rocks in the aisle and second pew of First Holy Baptist Church. She walks down that aisle every Sunday holding her baby close to her chest and sits in the second pew next to her mother, both their chins up, their eyes watching the pulpit, pretending not to feel the stones.

Our fellow stone thrower, Dorian, is cute. He's light skinned with sandy brown hair and light brown eyes. Normally Mona and Brandy would be all over him, tossing and twirling the thick, glossy hair that flops down their backs. But he walks with a limp, said his left leg is a little shorter than his right. That's fine by me. His legs don't have anything to do with his lips. Well, I don't think so, anyway. And beggars can't be choosers. I know I'm not the finest thing in the world. I've got skinny legs, no titties, no booty, a lanky body, and a large gap between my two front teeth. My face is okay, though, and when I smile with my lips pressed together, I know I'm not ugly. So all week, while we've been throwing pretend stones, I've been smiling toward Dorian with my lips pressed together.

That's how I've been smiling for all the pictures today, too. Since today is the last day, everyone is snapping pictures with their throwaway cameras, mostly taking group shots: guys trying to look cool like Jodeci and girls trying to look fly like En Vogue. Some take shots of two people, posing like they're at the prom, or three people in the case of Mona and Brandy. All the guys want a picture with Mona and Brandy.

Dorian is walking toward us now. We're backstage waiting for our part in the play. He asks us to take a picture with him, but Keisha, Mona, and Brandy are in it, too, so I don't feel special. But I *do* get to be closest to him, and now he *is* sitting next to me. He just pushed the Play button on his Walkman. He's singing, "'Put on your red dress. And slip on your high heels.'" I love that Johnny Gill song. *Is he singing to me?*

"Taja. Girl!" Keisha whispers in my opposite ear, bumping her knee against mine. *I guess he is singing to me.* I grab his hand. I know it's fast, but I need my kiss. I don't even have to tell you how fast my heart is beating, fast as Flo-Jo. He stands up, still holding my hand, and I follow him backstage through teens dressed as Bloods, Crips, preachers, teachers, drug dealers, crackheads, babies, and young mothers, then down some stairs.

The stairwell is bright and empty. We run down two flights before we stop. We can still hear the play being performed above us. I smile big, showing the gap between my two front teeth. I cover my mouth with my hand, like I always do when my real smile slips out. He grabs my hand, pulls it away from my mouth, and puts his lips to mine, then his teeth to mine. I feel his tongue slip into my mouth for a second and taste the faint, sweet flavor of a grape Now and Later. But then my teeth start guarding my tongue, and I don't know how to stop them. He tries to get beyond them, turning his head every which way, but he can't. I think he's slow, too. He settles on my lips, but I quickly whip my head around because I hear loud, running footsteps. An even brighter light fills my eyes, and I see Brandy, Mona, and Keisha. Brandy and Mona are laughing at me, and Keisha's face is hiding behind her camera. My cheeks heat up, and I start to get mad. But Dorian laughs, so I laugh, too. My teeth are showing. I am feeling pretty. We are all laughing now. We look up as we hear our scene start, but don't run up the stairs. We can hear the director yelling for us, but we laugh louder. There is no one to throw stones or be stoned.

# On Your Marks

Naima's been at my school six months and she's on my last nerve. I hardly ever have to see her because we live in completely different worlds. But in the middle of the day, fourth period, when I have track practice and she has PE, there she is, in my world, on my track, showing off in front of my team.

She's running around the track now, her puffy hair trailing, looking as if she's snatched one of the cumulus clouds out of the sky, dyed it black, and slapped it onto the back of her head. I don't know how many times I have to tell that girl to put her hair in a ponytail.

But no, she wants to wear her hair down because Flo-Jo wears hers down. Naima doesn't even have a perm. Her hair can't stretch long like Flo-Jo's, like mine. She even paints her nails like Flo-Jo's with colorful waves, dots, and stripes, prays for her nails to grow every single night. (I hear her beneath me, on her knees, before she climbs in the bottom bunk.) But her nails can't grow long like Flo-Jo's, like mine.

Naima has Flo-Jo's muscles, though, I'll admit. From the middle of the field, where the track team is stretching, I watch them flex. I wish I had muscles. Maybe then I would still be Coach June's favorite. Maybe then Coach June would let me run a race. All I do is jump—long jump, triple jump, and high jump. That's all my lanky legs are good for. I'm not even fast enough to run the hurdles. And I refuse to run long distance. Long distance is for white girls.

"I can't wait to get Naima on the team next year," Coach June says. She is pacing the field in front of our outstretched legs in a green and purple tracksuit that swishes each time she steps. Girls on the team hate the sound. She wears a different color tracksuit every day—different color but same *swish*. I love the sound. It's like my mom in the kitchen scrubbing our stainless-steel sink with a steel wool pad. It's like me sliding the first sheet of paper off a stack of freshly copied papers in class. (Oh, the warmth and smell of freshly copied papers!)

On days when it's hard for me to keep up with my mind, it's like high winds rustling tall grass—*swish, swish, swish*.

"Why don't *you* have any of that speed, Taja?" Coach June says, shooting me a disgusted look before turning back to Naima.

Naima, Naima, Naima. Everything is always about Naima. *Naima makes me sick,* I think.

"We could use her this year, especially against Lacey Carr," Coach June says, this time darting LaToya a disgusted look. We all thought LaToya was the fastest girl in the district until she went up against Lacey. At every meet last year, Lacey beat LaToya, beat her bad, too. "If only Naima was a year older—"

"Dang! She ain't that fast! She ain't that special!" LaToya interrupts, not looking up from the leg she stretches over. Everyone looks at Coach June. Talking back to Coach June can earn you twenty extra laps after school.

Coach June turns to face LaToya. Her beady, blue eyes look happy enough to dance. "Oh, so you think you can beat her?"

"I know I can," LaToya snaps, screwing up her face.

"And if you can't, you owe me thirty laps!" Coach June turns and marches across the field to Naima's PE teacher, her curly blond mullet bouncing off her neck with each quick step.

LaToya jumps up and starts warming up with butt kicks and high knees. The front half of her hair is stacked high, with curls that start five inches in the air then cascade down toward her face like a waterfall. As she warms up, her curls bounce together as a unit, not a single curl moving out of its place.

"You got this, girl," Erica assures LaToya. She, too, has a waterfall, but hers is long and juts out from the right side of her head, covering her ear.

"Yeah, you can beat her easy, girl," Courtney chimes in. Courtney's hair couldn't make a waterfall even if it wanted to; it's too silky. She's mixed with something, but I forget what.

Coach June motions for LaToya to meet her at the one-hundred-meter mark. She is walking and talking with Naima. She puts her arm around Naima. I have only seen Coach June put her arm around one girl and that was LaToya, before she got beat by Lacey. She's never put her arm around me.

*That's why I hope you lose*, I think, looking at Naima. But after I think it, I don't like myself. Naima gets on my nerves, but she is still my little sister, still my blood. I should want her to win. I search for the part of me that wants to root for her—the part of me that is part of her, too—but I can't find it.

They line up where the straight lanes of the track break away from the loop and go off on their own until the chain-link fence stops them. LaToya starts in the three-point stance

Coach June taught us: left leg forward, right leg back, right fingertips on the ground, and left arm stretched back. Naima starts with both her right foot and arm forward, her right arm bent like the muscular one on the baking soda box in our fridge. She doesn't know any better, and part of me wants to go show her the proper position.

"On your marks. Get set. Ready. Go!" screams Coach June. LaToya jumps out early. Naima's whole PE class is cheering her on from the bleachers. I look on in silence. The different parts of me are battling too hard to shout or clap for Naima. A few strides into the race, Naima catches up with LaToya. They run in stride with one another for a few yards, but then Naima passes LaToya. By the time Naima gets to the finish line, LaToya is two body lengths behind.

The PE class erupts into cheers, and I cheer with them because it would be weird if I didn't. I am relieved because part of me is actually happy for Naima, but there is still the other part that wants her victory to be mine. I run to congratulate the happy winner—like she would expect her big sister to do—but Coach June beats me to her and lifts her up like she's her child. I want to scream, "That's *my* sister! Put her down!" But I know that would sound stupid, so I turn around. As I turn, I see LaToya out of the corner of my eye and hurry my feet because I'm scared of the humiliation I know walks behind me.

When I get back to the track team, everyone is talking about LaToya, even Erica and Courtney. Brenda is the only quiet one. She throws the shot put, never says anything about anybody behind their back. If she has something to say, she says it to their face. Erica and Courtney start shushing the other girls when they see LaToya coming.

When LaToya reaches us, she says, "That was nothing. I can beat that bush-headed girl any day of the week, any day I feel like it, any day I actually try." The other girls laugh, but I don't because I feel funny about LaToya calling my sister "bush-headed."

"Are you going to let her dog your sister like that?" Brenda asks, curly eyebrows raised.

"I don't care," I say out of habit. But as soon as I speak the words, I feel ashamed. I've pretended not to care about put-downs directed toward me, but I can feel from the pounding in my chest that *I don't care* won't be enough for my sister.

"If I were you, I wouldn't let nobody talk about my sister like that," Brenda says, her large nostrils flaring.

The pounding in my chest gets hard, like the arm on the baking soda box is trapped inside and fighting its way out. "What did you say about my sister?" I yell at LaToya. The muscular arm drops from my chest to my stomach. Part of me feels afraid, but a bigger part feels strong.

"I *said*, yo ugly, bush-headed, gap-toothed sister can't run worth shit!" LaToya yells back.

*Oh, no, she didn't just talk about our gaps*, I think just before the muscular arm joins with my skinny arm and pops LaToya dead in the mouth. I feel her wet lips against the skin of my knuckles, her hard teeth against my bones. LaToya falls back in the grass with her mouth hanging open. Everybody's mouth is hanging open. My mouth is hanging open, but I close it quickly. With my skinny arm still bent in the air and LaToya on the ground, I search my mind for words to keep her down, but I don't have any sayings for this situation. I don't have a smart, quick mouth.

I hear footsteps close behind me and get ready for Coach June to yank me away, but instead, I feel Naima's soft bush rub against my shoulder and hear, "Jump up and get beat down!"—the very words I would have liked to say.

# The Good News

I shouldn't even be in Express. Mom gave me explicit orders to go straight into Palais Royal, pick up the dress she has on layaway, and come straight out. She's waiting in the car with Naima. The Easter Eve celebration began five minutes ago.

But no, I just *had* to walk by Express. And I just *had* to listen to the pair of yellow jean shorts in the window calling my name—*Taja, Taja*—and go in. Found them on a rack in the middle of the floor and looked at a tag. $34.95. April, May, June, July. Maybe they'd be marked down to $19.95 by July sixteenth—my birthday.

It's time to go. I turn to leave and right there on the

wooden bench facing the entrance are three boys. I missed them coming in. I have to walk right past them to get out. But I can't.

There's something wrong with my walk when I'm alone and have to walk past a group of boys. They don't even have to be cute boys. In fact, most of the time, they're ugly. And stupid. Stupid, ugly boys hanging by the pay phone outside the corner store when I want candy, stretched out across lockers like a chain of paper dolls when I'm late to class, perched on the roofs of cars in the parking lot after track meets, and sprawled out in the last pew of the church when my bladder won't take no for an answer and I have to excuse myself with my head slightly bowed and my first finger held up to the Lord. They're everywhere, these stupid, ugly boys. Judging me. Making everywhere I walk feel like a runway. But I'm no model.

I move to a side rack, away from the entrance, and thumb through shirts marked with red tags still waiting for someone to lift them up and take them home. I lift one up, put it to my chest, and look in the mirror so that if the boys are watching me, I will look like I'm really shopping. At least my hair is cute. I have it in a French roll. I smile at myself in the mirror. I can't help it. I smile all the time now that my new braces have closed my gap. Oh, my God! What if they just saw me smile at myself? They'll think I'm crazy. I *am* crazy. What am I doing? They're probably not even worried about me. They probably didn't even notice me to begin with. I start thumbing through the shirts, hard and fast, trying to crush my craziness with the clatter of metal hooks scraping the metal rack, plastic hangers banging their plastic neighbors.

I have to get out of here. I have to get Mom's dress. I know she's wondering where I am. I should have let Naima come with me. I should have ridden with Daddy. He left us after Mom took off her third dress. He couldn't be late. He's singing with the men's choir tonight.

I walk toward the front of the store along the side wall. I peek through the display window around the mannequin's skinny legs in my yellow shorts—*Are my legs that skinny?*—to see if the boys are still there. Dang it!

The two boys sitting on the ends are looking at their pagers. The one in the middle doesn't have a pager—well, not in his hand and not on his hip. He's cute and I imagine him kissing my lips. Even if it's only my bottom one, even if it's only a slight touch, like the way his upper lip brushes his lower one as he chews gum. I wonder what flavor it is. I bet grape, like the jelly that kisses peanut butter between bread before I take it out of its brown paper bag—same shade as the cute boy's skin. A tall lady in blue jeans stops right in front of the cute boy and blocks my view. Of all the places to stop, she had to stop right—wait! That's Mom!

I hide in the front corner of the store as Mom walks into Express with Naima. Naima carries the Palais Royal dress bag in her arms like a limp child. She twirls a few times, the red fabric hanging out of the bag over her arm like dangling feet. Mom walks fast and Naima runs to catch up. Naima is smiling wide, showing the green rubber bands around the metal on her teeth. Nothing makes her happier than to know I am in trouble. They walk toward the rear of the store, while I dash for the doorway, almost colliding with a fat lady in a royal blue dress. I don't have time to give apologies. I'm dead if Mom catches me in Express.

Leaving the store, I glance at the cute boy. His dimples hit the corner of my eye. I turn my head and smile. I'm walking fast, normal. Too scared of getting caught to be self-conscious of my walk.

"Oooweee, she got booty," one of the boys with a pager says. My body tenses up. *Please don't start.*

"Dang, she nice and thick," says the other pager boy. I glare at him, turn back around, and start to limp  not a broken-leg limp, a confused limp. *Stop, please, stop.*

"Yeah, thick like a Luke dancer," the last voice from the bench joins in. It has to be the cute boy. I forget how to walk.

My left leg is in more of a hurry than my right. My arms don't know when to swing up and when to swing back, if they should swing together, or how to move with my legs. I slow down, speed up; nothing works. I'm only halfway down the hall. I wish I could close my eyes, click my heels three times, and be back in the car.

"Taja!" I hear someone call. I turn around. It's Mom. Panic replaces confusion. I stop walking and start working on my story.

I had to go to the bathroom—bad. Saw a girl from school on the way back. Told her about the Easter Eve celebration. She said, *Have a good time celebrating Jesus's birth.* So sad, the poor girl had clearly never been to church. I said, *Jesus died, was crucified, but Mary Magdalene found an empty tomb, and on the third day God lifted Jesus up and took him home.* How can I get in trouble for that?

"Where the hell have you been?" Mom says, approaching. She's mad but not that mad. *Hell* is her only curse word, and she only uses it when she wants to sound madder than she really is.

"I had to go to the bathroom. Saw this girl from student council," I say, putting on my most innocent face. No need to bring God into my story, out of His resting place.

"We're half an hour late!" Mom says, grabbing my arm

without slowing her pace. I'm happy to have her stride forced upon mine. Her big booty cheeks always swing wide from side to side. I didn't realize my booty had grown big. I wonder if my big cheeks are swinging. I didn't realize I had gotten thick. I wonder if the boys are still watching.

"That's it? That's all she gets?" Naima asks, handing the Palais Royal bag to Mom. Mom takes the bag, swings it over her shoulder, and starts rummaging through her purse for the keys. When we turn the corner, I twist my neck and strain my eyes as far as they can see. No boys anywhere in sight. The wooden bench is empty.

*No need to hurry.*

*No need to sparkle.*

*No need to be anybody but oneself.*

—Virginia Woolf, *A Room of One's Own*

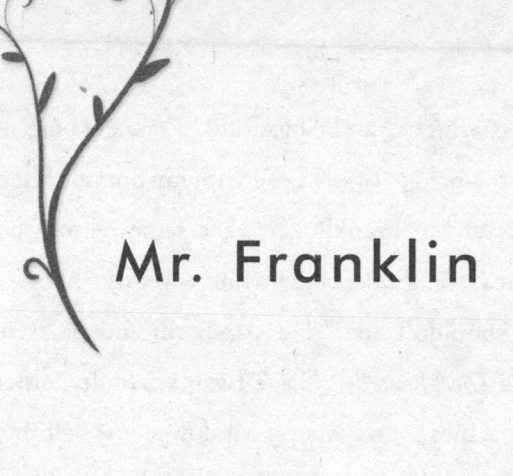

# Mr. Franklin

Honors English. First period. Fourth week. I'm sitting in the front row, my love transparent. *Call on me. I beg you. Call my name.*

"Taja," Mr. Franklin says. My vision of him is a little blurry through my new glasses, but I can still see him sitting on top of his desk, holding his coffee mug, with his long legs stretched to the floor and his slim-fit pants hiked just high enough to expose his polka-dotted socks. He wears cool socks every day: bold stripes, zigzags, and funky plaids.

"The milk and the Shirley Temple cup represent Pecola's

desire to be white . . . to be beautiful," I say, and push my new glasses up the bridge of my nose with my pointer finger.

"Yes," says Mr. Franklin. "It's the same reason she prays for blue eyes. She thinks being white will make her beautiful. And why shouldn't she?" He stands up and picks up Toni Morrison's *The Bluest Eye*. "Page twenty: 'Adults, older girls, shops, magazines, newspapers, window signs—all the world had agreed that a blue-eyed, yellow-haired, pink-skinned doll was what every girl child treasured.'"

He's walking down the far aisle, closest to his desk, one strong hand holding his book and the other hand playing with his push-button pen. His back is straight, and his baby face is serious. "Tonight, as you watch television or listen to the radio or read a magazine, pay attention to what you hear and see, pay attention to what people are telling you to treasure."

My eyes follow him as he starts up the middle aisle, only one aisle away from mine. I take my elbows off my desk and the roundness out of my shoulders.

"I want you to think about messages that might make you feel ugly, dumb, too tall, too short, too young, too old, too skinny, too fat, too good, too bad," he continues. He's almost to the end of the aisle, almost about to turn the corner and start down my aisle. "Anything that causes you to doubt yourself."

I sit up even straighter and push my new glasses farther up the bridge of my nose. I tried on the brown, square-framed glasses last night in Walgreens while waiting for Mom to pick out her panty hose. My reflection in the small mirror looked smart, mature. *Mr. Franklin will love them*, I thought, and put them in Mom's blue basket. "I get headaches when I read too long," I lied. Mom picked them up, looked at the $9.99 price tag, and allowed them to stay.

"And challenge it," Mr. Franklin tells the class, and starts down my aisle.

I look up at him through the thick, magnifying lenses and wait for his eyes to meet mine.

"Question it." And he walks past me, without looking down.

I pass Mr. Franklin's classroom, walk to the end of the hall, and turn around. Between periods, before school, and after school, Mr. Franklin usually stands outside his classroom talking to students. But today I haven't seen him since first period.

I want him to see my new glasses up close. It's hard to teach and notice glasses at the same time. When he sees me with glasses, he'll know I'm mature enough for us to be together. Obviously we can't be boyfriend and girlfriend right now (he's twenty-three . . . everyone asked him the first day of school), but we can still take it slow and start as friends.

When I reach his classroom again, I stop and wonder if he's in there. I can't see inside because he's covered the long rectangular window on his door with craft paper that says:

Steal.
Tell.
Overhear.
Reveal.
Yours.

My new glasses are impossible to read in, but I know what it says by heart. Each time I pass his classroom throughout the day, I read the sign like it's a gift. He wrote the same words on my first creative writing assignment along with a note that said, "You're a beautiful writer. Never forget that." I don't ever remember feeling so proud.

"Dang, *again*?" someone yells down the hall. I look and it's LaToya, minus her normal crew, Erica and Courtney.

Other than her, the hall is empty. School let out over twenty minutes ago. Still, I lean back against the beige-painted brick wall and pretend she's talking to someone else.

"And what's up with those stupid-looking glasses?" she says, walking closer.

I know she can't see my eyes, but I roll them anyway.

"You know they have laws against stalking?" She approaches with hot-pink lips and matching hot-pink shorts, baring manlike hairy legs. Her legs are gross, but she's worn them with pride since seventh grade. Now they're her signature. Other girls at school actually try to grow the hair out on their legs, but none can match the thickness and length of LaToya's.

I want to tell her to shut up, but I say, "I left a book in Mr. Franklin's classroom," hoping it will make her leave me alone.

"Liar," she replies, and walks past me.

*Finally*, and I exhale hard. *Wait*. She approaches the lockers along the opposite wall. Right, left, right, click, and she opens her locker, right there, in front of Mr. Franklin's classroom. I had no idea.

"You can stop frontin'. I see you walk past here a thousand times a day. Not my type, but he's all right."

"I don't know what you're talking about," I say, push myself away from the wall, and stand up. I probably still have time to catch Damon for a ride home. He always hangs out late in the seniors' lounge to talk to girls.

"Wait a minute," she says, voice high and bright. "Is that why you're wearing those fake-ass glasses? To look smart for your favorite English teacher? Probably got them things from Walgreens or somewhere."

The latch on Mr. Franklin's door clicks, and the door swings open toward me.

"Hey, Mr. Franklin," LaToya says, and shuts her locker.

"Hey, LaToya," Mr. Franklin replies, and walks away from me, past her, with his stainless-steel coffee mug in hand.

"I got something to tell you," LaToya says in a singsong voice, looks back at me, and walks to catch up with Mr. Franklin.

Mr. Franklin stops.

*She wouldn't*, I think. *She would*. I panic. *Say something, Taja. Anything.*

"Hey, Mr. Franklin," I call out.

Mr. Franklin turns and looks at me. "Oh, hey, Taja. I didn't even see you back there."

"I have a question about something you said in class today," I say.

"Y'all walk with me," he says, and starts down the hall again.

I run to catch up and walk on his other side.

"I was thinking about writing a poem," LaToya says.

"That's great," Mr. Franklin tells her. "Do you know what kind of poem you would like to write?"

"A love poem," she replies, leans forward a little, and cuts her eyes at me.

"I was thinking of writing a poem, too," I say, to stop LaToya from saying anything else. "I want to be a writer." The words feel weird coming out, like they belong to someone else. I've never spoken them or even thought them before. But the way my insides are dancing makes me change my mind, makes me feel like the words are mine.

"Yeah, me, too," LaToya says.

*Such a liar.*

"You both would be great writers," Mr. Franklin says, and opens the door to the teachers' lounge.

*I know he's only talking about me. He can't possibly think LaToya would be a good writer.*

The teachers' lounge is empty and he invites us in. I've never been in here before. It's a rectangular room with four large round tables in the middle and two small square tables back near the window. There's a refrigerator, a coffee maker, a vending machine, a Coke machine, and a huge bulletin board with colorful flyers. An orange flyer has a picture of a bike. I walk closer to the flyer to see how much it is, but I can't make out the numbers. On the back wall, near the window, there's a poster with white words printed over tall trees and a blue sky. I walk closer to it, stare at it, wishing I could read it. I think about taking off my glasses—they're giving me a headache—but Mr. Franklin hasn't noticed them yet.

Mr. Franklin finishes refilling his coffee mug and sits down at a round table.

I turn to face him and push the frames up the bridge of my nose.

"Did you get new glasses?" *Yes! He finally noticed.*

"Yeah, I can see much better now," I lie.

"Well, they look—"

"Or an astronaut," LaToya interrupts, and puts two quarters in the Coke machine. "Sometimes I think about being one of those, too." A can comes tumbling down. She gets the red can out, pulls back on the silver tab, and cracks the top open. "Or sometimes a hairdresser," she says, and pats the stack of hair jutting out from the left side of her head.

*Would you please just shut up.*

"It's okay to be unsure," says Mr. Franklin, and sips his coffee. "You just have to keep following what you like . . . keep doing your best . . . keep being yourself. As a matter of fact, Taja, would you read that poster back there?"

*No!* I panic. The white letters all run together and fade into the blue sky.

"Any day now," LaToya says.

I step closer to the poster . . . even closer . . . so close its smell is in my nose . . . perfume . . . floral perfume. The smell makes me feel sick and I back up.

"You mean you can't read with your *new* glasses?" LaToya says.

Tears start forming in my eyes, and I squeeze them shut, fight back the tears. I wish I could somehow make myself disappear.

"Maybe you should try to read it without the glasses," says Mr. Franklin.

*Wait, does he know?* I look back at him.

He nods his head. "Just try without the glasses," he tells me, raises his thick brows, and gives me a small smile that says he knows.

Embarrassment wants to rush in, but the way Mr. Franklin looks at me—not sorry for me or disappointed or annoyed—won't let it. I take off the glasses, fold them, and turn around. Relieved to be able to see again, I read:

Beauty begins the moment you decide to be yourself.
      —Coco Chanel

I stare at the words—*decide to be yourself*—repeating them in my head over and over again.

The metal legs of a chair scrape against the floor. "Ms.

Maggie just put that up today," says Mr. Franklin. (Ms. Maggie is the art teacher who always wears the cutest shoes and loudest perfume.) "I don't think there are many things in life more true." He starts walking toward the door.

"Well, then, I know I'm beautiful," LaToya says, downs the last of her Coke, lets out a small burp, and tosses the empty can in the trash.

Mr. Franklin opens the door and LaToya walks through. He holds the door open for me.

As I get closer, I see a sign on the side of the fridge that says "Lost and Found." On the countertop, just beneath the sign, there's a blue crate. I toss the brown frames in the crate, look up at Mr. Franklin, and we lock eyes—*Oh, my gosh! Oh, my gosh! Oh, my gosh!*— before I walk through the door.

# Lost It

"**W**eren't you were supposed to mail this last month?" I say, picking up Damon's UT college application from the front passenger seat of his car after school. The University of Texas is Damon's dream school, where all his friends will be. I reach to put the application on the backseat, but it's a mess: cleats, chip bags, McDonald's trash, his dirty baseball uniform, and fountain drink cups. Don't want his dream school getting lost in that nastiness, so I place it on the dashboard.

"I'm not stressing it. That's just for early decision."

I remember Mom talking to Damon about the importance of applying for early decision to increase his chances of getting accepted, but I'm too cold to ask any more questions. "Turn on the heat," I say, and rub my hands together before putting on my seat belt. "It's freezing." I exhale hard and watch my breath form a white cloud.

"Where's the CD?" Damon stabs the Play button on his car stereo, but there's no sound.

"I lost it," I say, shrugging my shoulders.

Damon looks at me, thick eyebrows folding. "Damn, Taja. Next time you——"

"Boy, I'm playing. I have your CD right here." I take off my seat belt and fumble through my backpack, between my feet, for my portable CD player. "Dang!" I say, spotting Mr. Franklin's book. He let me borrow it a month ago. Told me to have it back to him before Christmas break. Although I finished the book after two weeks, I kept it so my fingers could keep touching the pages his fingers had touched. So my face and lips could keep touching the places his hands had touched. Each night before I went to sleep, I put my cheek to its cover and laid the book on my desk, where I'd wake up to it in the morning and kiss it before putting it in my backpack.

"What? You better not have scratched it." He stretches his neck to look down at me pulling the player out of the backpack.

I pop the top open, take the Boyz II Men CD out, and hand it to him. "See . . . safe and sound, but I need to take this book,"

I say, and I pull out *Go Tell It on the Mountain*, "back to one of my teachers. I promised I wouldn't keep it over the break."

"Don't be all day," he says, and turns on the heat. Cold air comes blasting out, and he turns it down.

"Yeah, yeah, yeah," I tease, open the door, and step outside. A cold gust of wind smacks my face, and I clutch the book to my chest and take off running through the parking lot, across the school yard, into the school (heat, glorious heat), past the cafeteria, down the hall, past the principal's office, and down another hall to Mr. Franklin's classroom. The door's open but he's not here. I'll leave him a quick note.

Breathing hard, I look for a stack of sticky notes among the stacks of books on his desk. None. I look for loose-leaf paper. None. I see a spiral notebook, opened to a mostly blank page, only the word *January* written in large letters on the top line. I pick up the notebook, turn the page, and see the word *love* written vertically in tiny letters in the upper right-hand corner. *Love.* I run my fingers over the letters. *Could he have been thinking of me?*

My heart lights up and blazes beneath my coat. I unzip it. *Love.* The word makes my insides feel like they're dancing and singing around a fire. *Love.* Burning up, I take off my coat and throw it on a desk in the front row.

*Don't be all day*, Damon echoes in my head, and I quickly

turn the page, tear out a blank sheet from the spiral notebook, fold the ripped out sheet vertically along the fringe, scrape the folded edge with my fingernail from top to bottom, and tear off the fringe. *What should I say?* But I don't have time to think, so I write:

*Mr. Franklin,*

*Thanks for letting me borrow the book. I really*
*liked it.*

*The main character has questions about church*
*just like me.*

*Maybe I can talk to you about it after the break.*
*Hope you have a good Christmas and New Year.*

*Love,*

*Taja*

Wait, did I just write *love*? Maybe I should've used a different word in case the *love* he wrote wasn't about me. But I'm sure it is. Who else would it be for? I need to hurry. Chest pounding, I fold the letter twice and slip it into the middle of the book. I'm about to leave the book on his desk when I notice his coffee mug missing. *The teachers' lounge!* I don't know why I didn't think of that sooner.

I take the book and run with it down the hall. When I get

to the door, I peek in through its rectangular window. The first thing I see is the open freezer door. And underneath, two bodies, just bodies, pressed together against the refrigerator door. The bodies are tangled: a hand with red polished fingernails grabbing a strong arm, a strong hand on the curve of a low back. Something inside me wants to run away, but I lean in, look closer. A stocking-covered leg slides up a khaki pant leg. The stocking-covered leg is wearing a black Mary Jane pump with a big bow cute. *Ms. Maggie!* My eyes follow the khaki pants down to yellow-and-brown polka-dotted socks. *Mr. Franklin.*

Heat rises up the back of my neck to my head and I scream. Throw the book at the window. Kick down the door. Run in and yell, "What in the hell is going on?" Turn over tables. Throw a chair at the vending machine. Tear down that stupid poster on the back wall that says, "Beauty begins the moment you decide to be yourself." And shout, "Well, how you like me now?"

But only in my head.

In real life, I back away from the door, from the tangled bodies, and walk back to the car.

"What took you so long?" Damon asks as soon as I get in and shut the door. The heat in the car is blasting. "And where's your coat?"

"I don't know," I reply.

"What do you mean you don't know? You just had it. And I thought you had to give back that book."

I picture my black pea coat slung on the desk in the front row, feel heat rising behind my eyes, and say, "I said I don't know," to push the tears back down.

"What's your problem? You know Mom is gonna be mad about that coat. You need to go get it."

"And you know Mom is gonna be mad about that college application, too, but I don't see you rushing to mail it." Getting in trouble for the coat can't make me feel any worse.

"Whatever." Damon puts the car in drive and speeds off.

After we pull out of the parking lot and drive down the street, where Damon reaches the speed of seventy, I crack the window and push the book out.

The back and front covers flap open, the pages in between flap like wings, and the note flies out of the book and up in the air like it's being pulled by a string. The book loses its fight against gravity quick, lands in a ditch. But the note jerks back and forth in the air, like it's trying to decide which way to go. It's going toward a truck's windshield. No, underneath a car. No, up in the air. No, where did it go?

# A Dirty Job

Lisa is a ho. Well, at least everybody at school says so. She's leaning her left elbow on top of Damon's black Maxima with her booty hanging out of black daisy dukes, yapping her loud, red mouth to Paula about what she wants to do to Damon on Valentine's Day. I wish she'd shut up. I can't stand thinking about him doing all of that nastiness.

I'm sitting on the passenger side of his car, waiting for him. He gave me the keys because his baseball practice always runs longer than my track practice. Lisa and Paula don't play sports, don't dance, don't cheer, don't play instruments, don't act, and don't sing. They have no business still being here.

"He's taking forever and a day to wash his ass," Lisa says to Paula, her voice muffled through the window. Had to take my arm out of the warm February sun to roll up the window when I saw them coming. "Maybe I should go give him a hand." They laugh and Lisa's big breasts, pressed against the glass of the passenger window, bounce in my face like Mom's used to when I'd lie on the kitchen counter with my head in the sink and she'd stand over me washing my hair. At least the window blocks Lisa's breasts. They probably smell—not sweet like Mom's, not like the cocoa butter on her skin or the incense that used to burn next to me on the windowsill—like sweat or cheap perfume.

"Maybe he already left," Paula says, smacking her gum, with her right sneaker hiked up on Damon's front bumper. She's always smacking. People say it's to bring attention to her mouth. I don't know why she would want to do that with those crowded, overlapping teeth.

"Hello! This is his car and his little sister is in it. You think he just left her here?" Lisa says.

*Oh, so she does see me.* I was beginning to think she was blind.

Lisa pushes away from the car, leaving a small *V*-shaped sweat patch from her breasts on the window. *Gross.* I wonder how much longer she's going to wait.

"I'm just saying—"

"You ain't saying nothing." Lisa walks around the car and stops in front of Paula's bony, outstretched leg. She looks at Paula, at Paula's leg, at Paula's dirty Puma resting on the bumper, and then back at Paula. Paula lifts her leg in the air like a gate arm at a railroad crossing, Lisa passes under, and Paula lowers her foot back onto the bumper.

Lisa walks to the driver's side and digs in her baby blue, vinyl Prada backpack purse, triangle upside down. *So fake*. Then she takes out a sheet of paper and holds a pen to her heart-shaped chin while gazing at the sky. After a few moments, she writes a note, folds it, kisses it, and slides it under the windshield wiper. Red wax spirals up from a small tube, glides onto her lips. Another kiss, this time for the windshield. As her lips touch the glass, she looks at me and winks. *Gross. I don't want your kiss, and neither does my brother*, I tell her with squinted eyes and curled-up lips.

Lisa walks away and Paula follows. After a couple of parking spaces, I turn on the windshield wipers. Lisa's lips smear. I push the button to squirt washer fluid. It helps but only a little. Again and again, I squirt the fluid and speed up the wipers. Soggy, jagged pieces of paper smear the windshield. Smudged red wax. Lisa turns and sees: no lips, no sweet words, no poetry—although I doubt there was poetry.

I notice a scrap of paper, trapped under the moving blade, with the word *love* in faded blue ink, and turn off the wipers.

"Cock blocker!" she screams. I look up, and she points her middle finger to the sky, smiles like she won, turns, and keeps walking. Look at her walk. Like she just rode a bike. Everybody knows what that means.

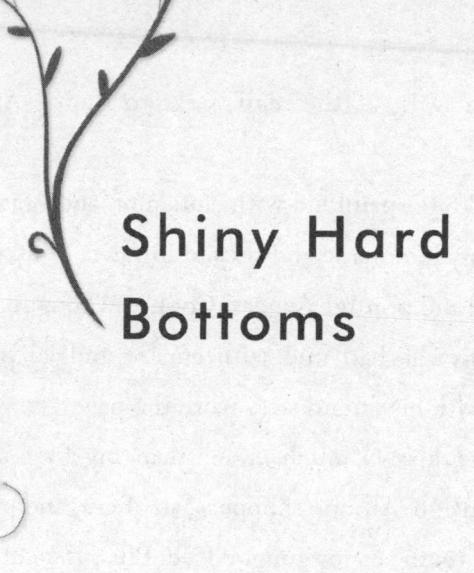

# Shiny Hard Bottoms

Keisha says I'm being naive. She's just mad because the cute boy wants me, not her. For once, her Chinese eyes don't make her prettier.

I can't even focus on kissing because Keisha's words, still playing in my head, make me keep glancing at her across the hall, a few stores down, foot on the wall, headphones on, like she doesn't know me. But it's not like she says. It's not my first time meeting him; well, maybe meeting him but not seeing him. I first saw him almost a year ago on the bench outside of Express, when I didn't pick up my mom's red dress. I'm kissing *him*.

Me. Against a wall, at the mall, next to Auntie Anne's pretzels.

We shared one sprinkled with cinnamon and sugar. He took a sip of my lemonade and sucked the sweet dusty mix off my middle and pointer fingers. Cool, wet tongue. Hot, wet tingles. Keisha had one with cheese and jalapenos; didn't share with his friend who wore the pager.

My second kiss is much easier than my first at the church convention. Among shoppers, strollers, and people watchers, my teeth set my tongue free. Plus, the cute boy isn't slow like me. His tongue rolls, licks, sucks, and slides down my neck easy like his words: smooth, slick as the hard bottoms of my shiny new church shoes.

"You're beautiful, Taja," he whispers.

Tiny balls of sugar grind the outside of my neck like the apricot scrub I use on my face when I get pimples— clean heart in my neck, dancing.

A little girl bumps into my right leg. A woman grabs her shoulders and guides her away, head shaking.

His tongue slides beneath my collarbone. Shopping bags pass. More heads shake. I pretend not to see.

Bite like a mosquito in the triangle above my collarbone. Foundation, powder, no ponytails for a week.

⬥ ⬥ ⬥

Gave me one last kiss on the lips with open eyes—I memorized a hundred shades of gold in that brown. Promised he'd call me that night. Waited. Waiting.

# Letters

**D**amon's going through the mail for the third time, sliding envelope after envelope out of the stack in his hand to the pile on the kitchen counter.

"It's okay. You'll hear from them soon," Mom says, washing Naima's hair at the kitchen sink. She's been telling Damon the same thing every day for the past two weeks . . . been telling herself, too. Since Damon received his fifth rejection letter (the last one from UT), we've been eating TV dinners.

"I'm just making sure," Damon says, still in his baseball uniform. Too bad swinging a bat and catching a ball haven't helped his chances.

"Which schools are you still waiting on?" I ask, and take a bite out of a Pink Lady apple.

"Just LSU," Damon says, and sits down on the stool beside me.

"And U of H," Mom says, squeezes a handful of conditioner out of the bottle, and puts it in Naima's hair. Naima's lying on the countertop, crying with her arms folded. At lunch today, she kicked a boy who cut her in line, and he turned around and dumped chocolate milk on her head. She claims it wasn't her fault, but the principal sent her home with a letter saying she'd have detention for three days.

"I'm home," Daddy calls from the front door.

"I don't want to go to U of H," Damon says, and puts his baseball hat on. "That's like going nowhere." He hangs his head low.

*Yeah, what's the point of going to college if you're going to stay in the same city*, I think. But I say, "You'll get into LSU," and take another bite. I'm not hungry, but I need a distraction from Damon's sadness.

Daddy comes into the kitchen, smelling like outside, and gives Mom a kiss on the cheek. "U of H is a good school, Damon," he says. He reaches around Mom and strokes Naima's wet hair, hanging down in the sink. "What's wrong with you?"

Naima looks up at him but doesn't say anything.

"Fight at school. I'll tell you about it later," Mom says.

"Okay, I'm going to get out of these clothes. . . . Hey, Taja," and he looks at me, smiles, and turns around. "No hats in the house," he says to Damon as he disappears out of the kitchen into their bedroom directly across the hall. The door shuts.

Damon says, "But—"

"Listen to your father," Mom says, cutting him off.

Damon takes off the cap. His eyes are red, like they're straining to push tears back. "I should've studied for my SATs. . . . I should've studied in general. . . . I could've made better grades. I should've mailed my—" He stops short of telling on himself and stops fighting the tears.

Mom leaves Naima at the sink and comes to put an arm around Damon.

At the dinner table, takeout pizza and Coke dry everyone's tears. I think Daddy even tells a few jokes because Damon and Naima are laughing. But I'm not listening, so I don't know. I keep picturing Damon's dream school application wasting away on the dashboard. Keep thinking about going to college. I want to go somewhere far away. Somewhere nobody knows my name.

I take a sip of Coke, feel itty-bitty bubbles breaking against my lips, and try to imagine such a place. All I can see is that poster of tall trees and a turquoise sky in the teachers' lounge. I think about Mr. Franklin (after hearing he proposed to Ms. Maggie over Christmas break, I forgave him . . . couldn't be mad at true love), about him telling me I'm a beautiful writer.

Tiny pangs of hope for my future prick the center of my chest. Forget *should've*s and *could've*s. I will do my best.

# Exalted
# Beginnings

I allow my eyes to play their tricks and watch the road ahead like a show: puddles dance in sequined skirts; harnessed waves rise from the asphalt, blurring the line where land meets sky.

"This is the beginning of your future," Daddy says, and turns to look at Damon sitting beside me on the backseat, his long, skinny fingers tapping his left knee. Naima's already asleep—mouth open, forehead pressed against the glass—which is exactly why I let her have the other window. Don't want her big head on my shoulder the whole way to Baton Rouge.

"The road, Jim," Mom says, whipping her half-moon face

toward Daddy. Her long chin almost meets her left shoulder. She and Daddy turn back to the asphalt at the same time, a black spine, yellow grass on either side—opened pages stretched flat to meet the blue sky.

"The beginning of the rest of your life," Daddy says, and turns again to look at Damon.

"Jim, the road." And this time Mom looks at him a few seconds after he turns back.

"Maybe I should've gone to U of H," Damon says, tapping his fingers harder against his knee. "At least I would have known somebody. I don't know anybody at LSU. What if I don't stand out? Those gumbo-fed Louisiana dudes are probably way bigger than me. And those long-haired Creole girls are probably all stuck-up."

"You need to be worried about your grades, not girls," Mom says, and looks at Damon longer and harder than she looked at Daddy. LSU admitted Damon on freshman probation, which means he needs to maintain a certain GPA his first semester to be readmitted the second semester. Mom and Daddy are making him go to summer school to get a head start.

I know Mom is right, but Damon is probably nervous about academics, too (probation can't possibly make him feel smart). Girls are just what he's comfortable talking about.

I want to touch his fingers, balled up in a muffled fist, but I know that would make him feel soft. So instead I say, "Boy, please. You know good and well those college girls will be sweating you. Don't ask me why. You're pretty ugly if you ask me. And your funky breath doesn't help."

Damon laughs, his left shoulder bouncing against my right, and rolls down his window. Air rushes in, fills up his T-shirt, and makes his chest puff up like a peacock's. Makes my ponytail rise off my shoulder and reach for the road ahead like it's the beginning of my future, too.

Somewhere along the road, high yellow grass turns to thick green groves and then to bare skinny trees, standing tall in swamps we cross on bridges. Each time we go over a bridge, it feels like a hundred baby birds stretch and flap their wings in my belly but don't have time to fly because the bridges are too short. I'm scared of the feeling at first, but I get used to it, and when we cross over the Mississippi River and the chicks flap and flap, and halfway across the bridge they lift off and fly over and through my twenty-four ribs, I don't mind because I know it must feel good to fly for the first time.

# Walls Can Wait

My new room is in the back of the house, facing the west sky, where I watch the sun scoot over each evening and find a fresh place to lie in the pine trees, where I listen to the fading sounds from the outside world float in and out of the window. My room, a new place for me to define, was baptized by the white coat Daddy and I painted on the walls—empty, waiting for the gold frames lying on the floors against the baseboards, bright, blank circles, squares, ovals and rectangles, ready to rise. We gilded them with gold leaf and rubbed them with glaze for an antique look after Daddy sat on the back deck carving them every evening for a week—hands steady, head moving to Coltrane. We'll hang them when I know what I want to live with. "What you love," Daddy said as I sat beside him on the deck. "Take your time."

*Love is like a virus.*

*It can happen to anybody at any time.*

—Maya Angelou, *The Heart of a Woman*

# Immunity Boost

**S**tarry circle on my mom's upper left arm, a vaccination scar from age fifteen. I push it hard like a broken elevator button to see if it will hurt. Face still in her book. *Guess not.* I make rings around it with my pinky to see if it will tickle. *Nope.* I stare at it hard, at all the tiny stars, to see if they hold any of her teenage secrets.

"Vaccines these days don't scar," she says, and swipes her sweaty bangs out of her long, oval face. Looks like the oval I stare at every morning in the mirror, only with more freckles.

"Promise?" I lean my arm into hers.

"Promise."

We are standing outside the clinic in line for a vaccine. School says I need a booster before starting school next week. Don't want anyone catching a contagious disease. Don't want anyone getting pregnant, either. Clinic has condoms in clear plastic bowls on folding tables outside its door. Colored circles trapped in clear squares, swimming. I strain my eyes to see. Won't lift my head an inch. Not a centimeter. Pretend to read. Mom is still reading. Didn't need condoms at my age. Didn't have sex until she was married. Still married. Followed all God's rules.

We follow in the line behind two heads with a million black ringlets. I follow too close and step on the back of one of the lady's shoes.

"I'm sorry," I say.

A girl looks back, kneels down, and fingers her sneaker back on.

A small "Humph" from Mom. The girl was supposed to say, "It's okay." "It's okay" would've been polite.

The girl turns around. Looks me up and down. The only invitation I need to do the same. Eyeliner on top lids, lips glossy—same as me. Tight T-shirt, holey jeans—same as me. Wait. Is she taller than me?

"Long jump, triple jump, high jump, right?" she says.

"Yeah," I say, and I tilt my head to the side. "How do you—"

"Me, too. Dulles High School. Red and black uniform. You're gold and green, right?"

"Wait. I know you. You always beat me in the long jump," I say.

"You always get me back in the triple."

"The high—"

"The high is always a toss-up. We'll see who gets the high this year when I'm wearing your gold and green—"

"Cassie," her mom calls, holding open the glass clinic door, and turns to talk to Mom, standing beside her. Busy chatting, Cassie and I forget to move with the line.

"My gold and green?" I ask.

"We moved. I'm going to your school this year," Cassie says, running backward, then turns around before she walks through the door, lifts a green condom out of the bowl like it's candy, and slips it in into her back pocket where there's a hole and green still shows. "Your turn," she yells, and disappears into the clinic.

*She did not just do that without getting caught!*

Cassie's mom finishes some words with my mom and follows Cassie inside. Mom grabs the door, holds it open for me. My turn. No, I can't. Don't dare. But when I pass the bowl of condoms, I turn my head and look at them with Mom standing right there.

# Cups of Tea

It's Christmas break and we're upstairs in Cassie's room sharing secrets about boys and sipping out of a red plastic cup filled with white wine she snuck from the room of women below, quietly exchanging their thoughts about books. Mom is still down there.

The first time Mom dropped me off to visit Cassie, she asked Cassie's mom, "So what church do y'all go to?"

"We don't go to church," Cassie's mom said, and finished pouring Mom's tea.

"Oh, I see," Mom replied, and stirred her tea, peppermint steam rising.

No tea for Cassie or me, only sugar cubes—sweet igloos washed away by the tides on my tongue.

Mom walked from the kitchen into the living room. I followed. She looked around and I looked around. Along open back windows, plants cascaded, climbed, and sat in rows on wooden stands like good students. Pearl walls were hung with frames displaying handwritten notes; pages torn from books; poems; pictures of Cassie and her mom standing in front of different houses, cars, and trees; cards; quotes; paintings of dancing women and drumming men, of faraway places with trains, tunnels, and clock towers—places I wanted to see. I left Mom to look closer. I wanted to hang written words on the walls of my room. I wanted to find pieces of the world worth framing in gold. I turned and saw a yellow bookshelf that lined a whole wall, books cheek to cheek. I wanted to read them all.

"Do you mind, Ms. James," said Mom, and grabbed a book off the shelf: *Jubilee*. She had just read it that week.

"Please, call me Anita."

Mom closed the book and squeezed it back on the shelf. "Well, I have to be on my way. Bible study starts in thirty minutes and I have to drive to Acres Homes. We attend First Holy on Piedmont Avenue, you know, across from the catfish stand. If you're looking for a church home, it's a great church.

You and Cassie would be more than welcome."

"Thanks. I'll keep that in mind. I saw you were interested in *Jubilee*. I hold a book club here on Friday evenings. Just women with an excuse to get together. You're welcome anytime."

Yeah, any time before tea turns to wine. I'm sleeping over at Cassie's house tonight. I give Mom a kiss good-bye after *Maud Martha*, the featured book, and two cups of tea. She opens the front door and says to call her if I want to come home. But I won't. I love Friday nights at Cassie's house, where women rock in chairs on the back porch while smoking skinny cigarettes, drinking wine from long-legged glasses, and loudly discussing books and men. Mom is gone. They only move to the back porch after Mom has gone.

# That Girl

"That girl wasn't anything special," Damon says.

"Who?" I say, but I already know. I'm just focused on applying another coat of plum polish to my big toe without messing it up for the third time—hard while holding the phone between my head and hunched shoulder.

"What's that sound?" Damon asks, annoyed.

"Oh, that's just Daddy. You know he started lessons after you left."

"I don't know how you take it."

I love hearing Daddy push notes out of his saxophone, no matter how off-key. "Hold on," and I put the polish down, get up, and carefully walk on my heels with my toes spread to close the door. As soon as door meets frame, Daddy's horn is replaced with the faint chorus of the neighborhood girls' favorite song:

*"Hollywood now swingin'*
*Hollywood now swingin'*
*Hollywood now swingin'*
*Hollywood now swingin'"*

They sing it to keep the double-Dutch rope swinging to a beat. After the chorus, the girl who's jumping always sings a sassy solo (I know because they double-Dutch like we used to play kickball—all the time). I strain to hear the solo, but can't. I walk toward the window, but still can't. It always starts with:

*"My name is _____."*

"Hello?" Damon says, sounding annoyed again.

"Yeah," and I sit back down.

"Anyways . . . that girl," he says.

What are the chances that Joanna, Cassie's cousin, who taught us how to pin-curl our hair, would also be a freshman at LSU? I love Joanna; she's cool. "Oh, yeah. What happened?" I ask, wiping the excess polish off the skin around my toenail. I stretch my legs out on the floor.

"Well, the first time I went over, she gave me a kiss. The second time, after her roommate finally left, she let me cop a feel. I almost hit the third time, but the roommate came in. The fourth time, I hit quick."

"Why do you have to make it sound like that?" I ask, imagining him in his dorm room, feet nonchalantly propped up on his desk, away from the dirty clothes, soda cans, and crumbs all over the floor.

"Like what?"

"I don't know. Like the way you're making it sound."

"Look, Taja, I'm trying to teach you a thing or two. I thought you were old enough for me to be straight up—"

"I am. I am." *But Joanna must have loved you*, I think, and imagine her staying up the night before, pin-curling her hair, tying it with a scarf, being careful not to sleep too wild, and before her date, separating the curls, side to side, bottom to top, like she taught. "So what happened next?"

"When?"

"On the fifth date? Was her outfit cute? How was her hair?" I ask.

"You don't get it. There was no fifth time. That girl was

easy," he says. "That's the problem with girls."

His words make my eyebrows crouch down, the left side of my lip curl up. *What about boys? What about you? God didn't say sex was only a sin for girls*, I want to say, and imagine him sitting on the floor in his filth, basking in the beam of light he must think God shines down on him. But I know better. Since Damon has been away at school, safely removed, he talks to me like a friend; he's even said on multiple occasions that I'm cool. Speaking my mind would be a quick step back to little sisterhood, so I hold the phone hush-mouthed, sell out Joanna.

"Don't be that girl, Taja. Don't ever be that girl."

*Too bad you're already that boy, who makes promises of love, but lies, lies, lies to get what he wants, and so easily convinces us we want the same thing. That boy who preys, makes us give, wish, hope, pray, then wait and wait and wait. That boy I hate.*

# The Hard Truth

*I swear if Naima is still on the phone with Alice.* I pick up the cordless receiver in my room . . . again. Hit the Talk button . . . again.

"Maybe," she says.

And before I can yell at her to get off the phone, a boy's voice: "Why maybe?"

*No, she didn't start a new conversation after I told her I needed the phone. And who is this boy?* I press Mute and lean back against my new, tufted headboard, made by Daddy, of course.

"Because," she says, in a soft voice, trying to be sexy.

"Because what?" His voice is low and soft, trying even harder.

"Because I said so."

"You already let me kiss you."

"And?" Naima's voice shoots high and loud.

He keeps his sexy voice on and says, "So if we kissed, then we should be together."

"Says who? It wasn't even that good."

A long pause.

I clutch my blue bedspread and wait for Naima to say she's joking, but she doesn't. I wish I could say it for her.

A loud and long sigh, like she's bored. Then, to top it off, she says, "I don't think this is gonna work."

"Why?" His voice sounds small, hurt.

"It's just not."

"But I love—"

"I gotta go," she says, and hangs up the phone.

Something inside me breaks for the boy. Breaks for me, too. For the times I've liked someone who didn't like me back. For the boy at the mall who tongued me down but never called.

Naima busts in my room and yells, "You better stop listening to my phone calls," over the sound of Daddy's saxophone. He's getting better.

"I wasn't," I lie because I don't like her telling me what I *better* do.

"Liar!" she says with a wild jerk of her head.

"You're a liar."

"Mom," Naima yells, and walks out.

I follow her into the kitchen, where Mom is cooking another casserole for some sick or old person. Since Damon's been gone, that's all she ever does.

"Taja keeps listening to my phone calls," Naima complains, and leans against the refrigerator.

"Do not." I walk past Naima and lean against the counter.

"Do, too."

"Hand me those, will you?" Mom says, pointing to a pair of oven mitts near the sink. "And stop listening to your sister's conversations."

I hand them to her and say, "It's not like I'm trying to listen. Every time I pick up the phone, she's on it. She *stays* on the phone."

"You can easily hang up when you hear I'm on it," Naima says.

Mom puts on the oven mitts, takes the casserole out of the oven, and places it on the stovetop. "I need the foil out of that drawer," and she points to the drawer between the oven and refrigerator.

"I need my own line," I say.

Naima hands Mom the foil, and Mom takes off the

mitts, tears off a few sheets, puts the mitts back on, and covers the casserole, pressing the edges down over the glass dish. "You know how your dad feels about that." Then she wraps the glass dish with dish towels and places it in a cardboard box. "Jim, can you come in here?" she yells.

Mom walks into the dining room and grabs her purse, hanging from a chair, and Daddy walks in.

"I need my own line," I say again.

"I shouldn't be too long," Mom says, and grabs the box with the casserole inside.

Daddy reaches to take the box from her.

"I got it," she says.

"Who's it for?" Daddy asks.

"Brother Lester . . . doctor gave him a month . . . might as well enjoy good food while he can," and she walks out of the kitchen. "Naima, come get the door for me."

As soon as Naima's gone, I say, "Daddy, I need my own line," using my sweet voice.

"You know we've already talked about that," he says, and touches my shoulder like that should make me feel better.

"But it's not fair. Damon had one when he was in high school."

He walks across the kitchen and gets a large glass mug out of the top cabinet near the refrigerator. "Damon's a boy."

"So?" I lean back against the wall and fold my arms.

He opens the freezer door. "I need to know who's calling here for you," he says, and pulls out an ice tray.

"You mean what *boys* are calling."

Holding both ends of the tray, he twists it, and the ice cubes pop up. "Yes."

"You never knew who was calling Damon."

"I didn't need to. Boys are different," he says, dropping cubes into his mug.

"Why does everybody keep acting like different rules apply for boys?"

Ice cracks in the glass as he fills his mug with water. "Because . . . well . . . you know I'm only trying to protect you, Taja."

"So boys can do whatever they want and girls have to follow all the rules?"

"I'm not saying that. It's just that—"

"Yeah, that's basically what you're saying. It's not fair!"

Naima comes back into the kitchen. "I can do whatever I want, too," she says, grabs the cordless receiver off the wall, and gives me the middle finger behind Daddy's head.

"Taja," Daddy says, and takes a sip of water. "That's just the way it is."

# Good Guides

At a red light, I look at Mom's directions to the house on my left palm: neat, blue letters written across long, swooping lines; four blue hearts on my calluses, one for every time she said, "Remember to *Spread the Love.*"

But what if I don't want to spread the love? I'm not that good of a person, certainly not as good as Mom. It seems reasonable to think that because I came out of her belly, sucked milk from her big breasts, obey all her rules, smack gum like her, smile wide like her, swing my hips from side to side like her, have a long chin like her and skinny ankles like her and fatty knees like her that I would at least approach her goodness. But I don't come close.

I follow my hand and take a right at the corner of South Victory Drive past a homeless man shaving his face on the corner. I've already made it to the neighborhood, Acres Homes. All I have to do now is find the woman's house, drop off this food, and pick up last week's casserole dish. It's not that hard.

But Mom didn't tell me the woman's affliction. What if she's old and dying? I turn left on Carver Road at a leaning stop sign.

It will only take ten minutes, ten minutes and I can go back home. I wish I could drive to Cassie's house, but Mom seems to think my learner's license is only good enough for her leftover errands (she had to attend Sister Elena's brother's funeral today). I step on the gas, drive fast past empty lots of overgrown grass, abandoned shacks, chain-link fences guarding wooden houses wincing under the orange sun. Occasionally I see people, old and alone, sitting on their porches staring back at me, looking like they could use some love.

But last Sunday and the Sunday before that and the Sunday before that, during the announcements, when Sister Davis asked the congregation, "Do you want to spread the love this summer?" did I say yes? Did I sign up? No, I didn't.

The road bends and I start looking for an old, red-brick

church, born again as a house. Mom said I wouldn't see an address but could find it easy if I looked for the steeple—a tall white cone topped with a steel cross—this must be it. I pull into the driveway behind a shark-gray Cutlass Supreme and turn the engine off. Next door a few men are in the front yard playing cards at a folding table, shouting and laughing over a boom box blaring the blues.

I wish they could tell me what sick, elderly, or shut-in woman will answer the door. I just hope it's nobody with a hunched back, nobody that smells like death or looks like death, nobody that wants a hug. I pray the dish is washed and she doesn't have roaches. If I see one scuttling behind the toaster, under the refrigerator, or across the kitchen floor, I will think one is somewhere on my body or in my hair and want to shake and shake and jump up and down, but I can't because I am a Brown child, the daughter of the head of the Sick and Shut-In Ministry, the daughter of a deacon, a representative for two important people.

*Come on, Taja, on the count of three.* One, two, and I grab the casserole off the front seat, swing open the car door, step out into the heat, slam it shut, and take six quick leaps on round, pebbled stepping stones to the creaky porch that leads to a screen door. Behind the screen, a white door with an arched, stained-glass window hangs wide open, but there is no sick yellow smell coming from inside—thank God.

I ring the bell and wait, sun thumping the back of my neck. Ring it again. Wait. This is about to be easier than I thought, because after the third ring, I'm gone.

"Coming," a deep voice calls.

Spatula in his hand, a man approaches the door. No, he has a body like a man, but a face like a boy. A cute one, about my age, in fact.

He pushes open the screen door, and I step back out of its way, try to steal another look without getting caught. The sleeves are ripped off of his football jersey, and his long shorts come past his knees, almost meeting his white socks. Holding open the screen door, his right biceps bulges like a bison's back. Wait, I don't see any hair under his arm. Does he shave? No, I see a few tiny, black curls—good, shaving his underarms would be strange. From hooded, light brown eyes, he's looking at me like I'm crazy. Oh, yeah, the food.

"I'm part of the *Spread the Love* program for First Holy Baptist Church," I say. Wait, did I just tell a lie on church ground? No, I may not have signed up for *Spread the Love*, but I still help out. "I'm here to drop off this casserole"—I hold up the glass bowl—"and pick up last week's dish."

"Oh, yeah, the one with spinach, chicken, and mushrooms. I tore that up. You made that?" he says.

"Not all of it, but I sautéed the mushrooms and seasoned the chicken."

"The mushrooms were nice and spicy. They set the whole thing off."

"Thanks."

"It's hot out here. You wanna come in?"

He extends his arm and I slide past—shoulder at his chest, forehead at his long chin. Dang, he's gotta be at least six feet five, because I'm five feet ten. Wait. Could he be the one with the affliction? Mom said it was a woman, but maybe she was confused. He walks ahead of me and I look close. No limp. All limbs seem to be the same length. No bumps on his head. No marks on his dark skin, which looks like the sun has kissed and kissed again.

"Moonie," a voice calls from a back room.

"Coming," he answers, and speeds up his walk. I follow behind him past the living room, which has an old church organ—I wish I could press a key, hear a sound—sitting between two stained-glass windows, and into the kitchen. With his spatula, he points to a pan of cornmeal-crusted fillets, way past golden, bobbing in boiling grease. "Can you take these out?" he says, lifting the casserole out of my hands and placing it on the counter behind him. He hands me the spatula. "Thanks," he says, and disappears around the corner.

I find a plate in the plastic rack beside the sink and line it with paper towels. I've seen Mom do this a million times. With the spatula, I lift the fillets out of the grease and lower them to the white blanket. One breaks apart: white, flaky. Looks like catfish—burnt, but still my favorite. Beside the stove, there's a plate of fish waiting their turn. I put them in the grease and watch the big, brown bubbles rise and pop, excited for fresh meat. The fish on the plate calls me one too many times, and I pinch off a corner of the smallest piece I can find.

"Ooh, I'm gonna tell," the cute boy sings, walking back into the kitchen, smiling with straight, long teeth.

I turn around and smile wide. "Tell, tell, your booty smell," I say, eat the piece of fish—dang, it's good—and stick my tongue between my thumb and first finger to lick off the crumbs.

"Oh, it's that good?" He pinches off a corner of the same piece and eats it. "That's what I'm talking about. Your boy has skills."

"I don't know about all that. Let me see," I say, and eat another piece, just to taste it again. "I guess you have a few skills. You cook a lot?"

"Just a couple times a week when I come over here. Grandma Betty loves her fried catfish. My mom says she shouldn't be eating this type of junk with her cancer and all, but I say, Hey, why not?"

I wasn't even hungry. I could have eaten when I got home. But no, I just had to be greedy with his grandmother's catfish, his sick grandmother's catfish, his dying grandmother's catfish. I can't even meet his eyes, so I turn back to the stove, flip the fillets in the grease, and wait on him to say he has it from here and take the spatula back. Wait on him to hand me the empty dish and send me on my way. Wait to feel stupid when I realize this safe space to be myself—my real self—this crazy good way our hearts are speaking is all in my head.

"What's your name?"

"Taja."

"Andre."

"I thought I heard your grandmother call you something like—"

"Moonie? Yeah." He turns his head to the side—more crescent shaped than mine.

"Me, too!" I say, and turn my head to the side.

He laughs and grabs my chin like it's an ice-cream cone.

I grab his chin the same way, and something strange starts spreading across my chest. Something delicious and unstoppable.

"You're crazy," he says, and we let go of each other's chins.

"Me?" I say, and take the fish out of the pan. Turn off the fire.

He puts two pieces of burnt catfish on a plate.

"These are better," I say, and point to the ones I've just taken out.

"It's cool," he says, pours some iced tea from a glass jug in the fridge, and grabs a bottle of hot sauce from the cabinet. "Wait here." He disappears around the corner.

Oh, my gosh! I am not this lucky. God is not this good. I wish I could do a cartwheel right here between the fridge and the stove. I wish I could bust out and sing, "Amazing Grace, how sweet the sound that saved a wretch like me!" I wish I could—

*Calm your butt down, Taja.*

Okay, but can you believe—

*Now.*

All right, all right. Deep breath in, deep breath out, and I find a dishrag draped on the sink faucet, busy myself with cleaning up.

Andre walks back into the kitchen, carrying a plate of half-eaten breakfast—eggs, toast, and grits. "Grandma Betty wants to meet you."

*Why?* I think. *She has her food. I did my job. Actually, I did more than my job.*

"She won't bite."

I fake-laugh to make up for the look I must have had on my face.

He puts the plate on the counter and says, "Come on."

I put down the rag and follow him around the corner, down a hall lined with three stained-glass windows—no figures, crosses, or scenes—three labyrinths of stars with bright panes of blue, yellow, red, and green, separated by black lines, traveling from point to point, not knowing where they are going or what they are forming or what color they will meet or where they are inside the maze or when they will hit the window frame.

I run my finger along a black line between the arms of a red and blue star, and try not to think of Gigi. Tears come and I blink them back.

I knew this would happen. I should have taken my butt home, escaped when I had the chance. But no, I just had to stay, had to let this Mac Tonight boy suck me in.

I keep placing one foot in front of the other and try not to think about the last time I saw her, about the weak hug I gave her, about how I was afraid of her oldness, her sickness, her pain.

Ahead of me, Andre turns in to an arched doorway—deep breath in, deep breath out—and I follow him into a room that smells sickly sweet. I stop breathing. On the far wall, hazy streams of yellow pour in through three stained-glass windows. In the corner, a large television plays *Wheel of Fortune*.

"*S!*" his grandmother says, lying at forty-five degrees in a hospital bed, red scarf around her head. The plate of burnt fish sits in her lap. A man standing behind the wheel chooses the letter *V*, a buzzer sounds, and the next person spins. "*V*? How stupid could he be?" she says, and turns toward us. I stop in the middle of the floor and Andre continues to the wooden pew at the foot of her bed. "He could have at least said *T* or even *R*, but *V*? He must not want his fortune. Shoot, give it me."

I laugh and breathe.

"Oh, you have to excuse me. I get a little beside myself when it comes to my game shows," she says, and takes a bite of burnt fish.

"Sorry your fish got burnt," I say.

"Child, please. Burnt makes you pretty. Why you think I look so good?"

I smile—hold it, hold it. Hoping what I see doesn't show on my face: ashy skin draped over hollow cheeks, legs like bones under thin white sheets—

"Come on over here so I can get a good look at you."

I pick up one foot, put it down. Pick up the other foot,

put it down. How many times? And I'm standing at her side.

"If you ain't your momma's twin, then somebody needs to come slap me."

I laugh.

"What is it with all these moon faces around here?"

I laugh again and see past sick and old to a funny woman who likes burnt fish and game shows. I notice my shoulders are hunched up and let them go.

"You're crazy, Grandma Betty," Andre says, turning around in the pew.

"I'll tell you what, Moonie—if any more moon faces show up here, just send them on down to Jessie's house. Just about everybody down there has a square face, ugly looking, too. They could use some moons down there," she says, and coughs.

Something about the way she makes me laugh won't let me feel sorry for her.

She grabs my pinky finger and says, "Tell your momma that I'm grateful. I am. One thing, though—can you tell her I don't like mushrooms? Last week's casserole had mushrooms. Moonie ate it but I don't eat mushrooms. Oh, no. Fungus makes you ugly."

"That must be how Andre, I mean Moonie, got so ugly," I say, and laugh.

She laughs and coughs and laughs.

"Oh, okay. I see somebody wants to clown," Andre says, laughing.

Grandma Betty squeezes my pinky tight, and says, "Thank you. You're a sweet, sweet child. Just like your mom." She lets go. "Moonie, now I already told you this in private, but I'm gonna say it again, so that—what's your name, child?"

"Taja."

"So that Taja can hear me—you better take good care of her."

A smile splits my face wide open.

Andre shakes his head and smiles, pursing his big curvy lips. "Time to go," he says, standing up. He touches my hand, I open it, and he slides his fingers inside mine and leads me toward the arched doorway. I look back. "*T*," Grandma Betty says, and the lady inside the television listens. *Bing*. A piece of the puzzle lights up, and Vanna White turns the letter before we turn the corner.

*The greatest lie ever told about love*

*is that it sets you free.*

—Zadie Smith, *On Beauty*

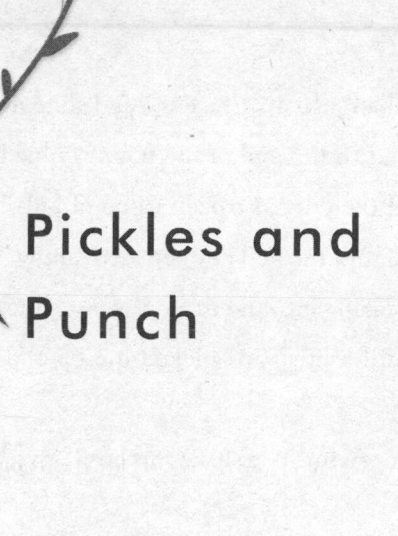

# Pickles and Punch

Andre and I are craving something sweet and sour. We walk to the corner store under the orange August sun and get a pickle and a Big Gulp—fill it with fruit punch. Don't put on a lid. I dip the pickle in the punch, take a bite, and say, "Oh, yeah." I dip it again and raise it to his mouth. He takes a bite and says, "That's what I'm talking about." At the cash register, I pretend to reach for the money in the pocket of my jean shorts. Andre pays and I thank him.

On the way back to my house, we walk past the neighborhood pool, full of screaming kids, and I tell him about my last time there. I was ten and wanted to dive in from up high rather than just sit at its edge and slide in. I climbed the ladder, walked to the end of the bouncy blue board until my toes touched the edge. I froze. A line of kids formed behind me, but I couldn't move. They kept screaming, "Jump! Jump!" But I stood staring into the turquoise sea, cracked with white lightning, until a lifeguard picked me up and carried me to the concrete.

"You can't swim?" He shakes his head, says, "Black people," and laughs.

"I can swim," I declare. "Took lessons and everything. I just froze that day."

He laughs again.

"What's so funny?" I want to know. "I haven't been able to get into a pool since."

He scoops me up and laughs, and whirls me around and laughs. My sandals fly off, and I hook my arms around his strong, sweaty neck, pickle and Big Gulp still in my hands.

Heat underneath my bare feet, I'm back on the ground, coughing up laughter. He waves his white T-shirt, wet with red punch, away from his back. "That's what you get," I say.

The pickle doesn't last long. I chew the last bite a few times before I offer it to him by sticking out my tongue—a test to see if he loves me. He brings his lips then tongue to mine, swipes the mush of sweet and sour, and swallows. "You're so nasty," I say, and smile.

On the sidewalk, we're careful not to step on cracks. Don't want to break our mothers' backs. He admits if it was his father's back, he wouldn't be so careful.

"I only met him once," Andre says. He walks slow, head down, ignoring the cracks. "I was eight, maybe nine. Mom woke me up in the middle of the night and brought me to see a tall man in the kitchen. He gave me a dollar and a high five and I went back to bed."

"That was it?"

"Yep."

I search myself for what he must be feeling, but I can't find that kind of sadness. That hollow, numb sadness. I want to push it away from him, so after a few silent steps, I point out his wet, red mustache and laugh and laugh, even though I know it's not funny. He doesn't laugh, so I leap in front of him, stand on my tiptoes, grab his upper lip with my lips, and suck the red juice off until his lip springs back.

There isn't much fruit punch left in the cup. We sip and pass and sip and pass. When all the red juice is gone, we suck on the chunks of ice. When they melt down to a digestible size, we chew and swallow—cold bits sliding down our throats—until we have nothing left but an empty Big Gulp.

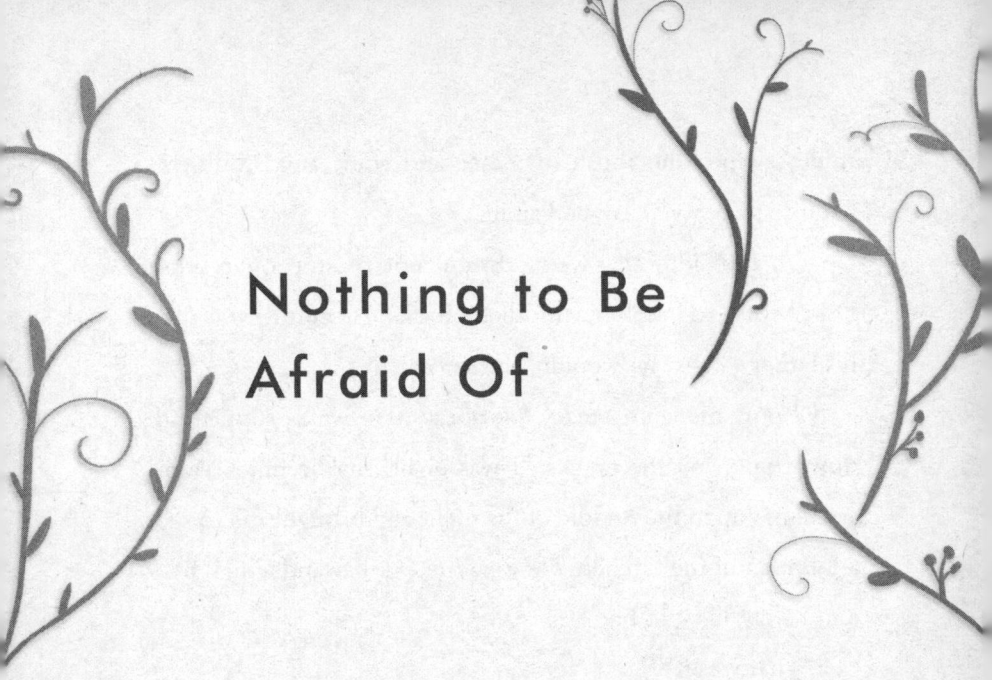

# Nothing to Be Afraid Of

At the dinner table, Daddy is full of new stories. About how he asked Mom out ten times before she said yes—she was hard to get. About how Grandpa (Mom's dad, who died when I was two) accompanied them on every date until they graduated high school, including school dances. Grandpa always volunteered to chaperone school dances to make sure they didn't dance too close to each other. The rule was Daddy needed to stay at least a foot away. If Grandpa ever thought Daddy was too close, he would take out his wooden ruler to measure.

Andre can't stop laughing. When I first told him my

parents wanted him over for dinner, he was scared.

"See, I told you there was nothing to worry about," I whisper in his ear, and grab his hand under the table. Daddy and Mom are sitting across from us. Naima's spending the night with a friend.

"Okay, time for dessert," Mom says, and stands up.

I let go of Andre's hand.

Mom takes our dirty plates to the kitchen and comes back carrying a large plate with four chocolate cupcakes.

Andre and I each take one. "Thanks, Mrs. Brown," Andre says. "I love chocolate."

Mom sets the plate down in the center of the table. "I know. Taja told me."

"Yeah. Thanks, Mom," I say, looking up at her, smiling about the cupcakes, smiling about my parents liking Andre and Andre liking my parents. I take a bite. "Y'all on a diet or something?" I ask, covering my full mouth. Both of their cupcakes are still in the center of the table.

"We have something for the both of you," Mom says, and walks out of the dining room.

"Presents!" Andre says, grinning.

Daddy smiles, but his round, soft eyes won't meet mine.

Mom walks back in carrying two scrolls, both held together by silver rings. "This one's for you," she says, and hands one to Andre, "and this one's for you." She hands one to me and sits down.

Andre and I slide the silver rings off the scrolls at the same time. The ring is a solid band with the words *true love waits* engraved around the exterior. A cut-out heart separates each word. *Cute.* I slide the silver band onto my left ring finger and imagine Andre and me standing at a wedding altar in the middle of a forest.

He looks over at me, smiles, and slides his ring on, too. "Thanks, Mr. and Mrs. Brown."

"Yeah, they're cute. Thanks," I say.

"You have to read the paper," Daddy says.

"Oh, okay," I say, unroll the paper, and hold it open. At the top, in bold letters: *Vow of Purity.* Immediately, I know what it is. I can't believe I was stupid enough to think they invited Andre over to get to know him better . . . to think they would give us sweets and gifts when it's all been about this.

In the top paragraph, I see the words *sex* and *Christ* and *virginity* and *purity* and *Jesus* and *souls.* In the middle, there's a scripture. And at the bottom, in bold, it says:

Purity Pledge:
I understand that having sex before marriage
is a sin, and that true love always pleases God.

From this day forward, I pledge to God, my family, my friends, and myself that I will keep my body and soul pure and abstain from sex until the day I am married.

Signature _____

Date _____

Andre kicks my foot under the table, and I think about how we play footsies in his bed when his mom is at work. About how just last night, in the car, he took off my bra, kissed my breasts, and touched me down there.

Daddy digs in his pocket and takes out two white pens with a cross in the center. "We know y'all are spending a lot of time together . . . developing strong feelings for each other. Your mom and I understand . . . we've been there. This is just to help you set boundaries. Having sex doesn't just happen. It's a choice. But it's also a sin. And you know God has consequences for sin. You can't forget that, even with all of these new feelings." He reaches across the table and places a pen in front of each of us.

Andre picks up the pen right away, signs, and dates. Must be easy for him to sign a contract he already wants to break. Him and his mom don't even go to church. When he was little, he occasionally went with his grandmother, but that's it.

I stare at the pen. Don't want to pick it up. Don't want to sign a contract with God. "I can't," I say, heart beating fast. *What if I break it? What would God do to me?*

Daddy's eyebrows crumple. "And why not?"

"I'm still a virgin," I assure Daddy. I can't believe those words just came out of my mouth. Can't believe I'm talking about my sex life to my parents. I look down and say, "And I plan to stay that way. I just don't feel comfortable with the whole pledge thing. It's so extreme."

"Extreme? We're talking about your life, Taja. Your relationship with God—"

"You don't have to sign if you don't want to," Mom interrupts. "But there's nothing to be afraid of. You're just pledging to continue to love God and honor yourself and Andre until . . . if . . . or when you're ready for marriage."

I wonder if they made Damon sign one. I seriously doubt it, but I pick up the pen anyway. There's no point in going back and forth when I don't have a choice. No matter what Mom says, I know if I want to keep seeing Andre, if I want to keep the bit of freedom I have, I'd better sign.

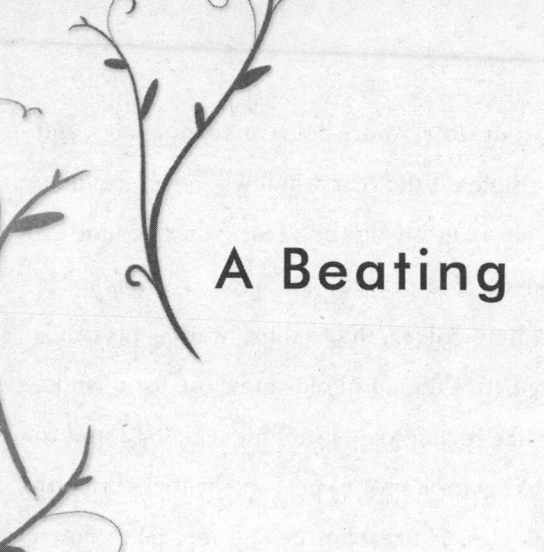

# A Beating

I can't stop looking at the Bible. We kiss. There, on the back-window ledge of the car, in the light of the moon. And kiss. Corners of its burgundy cover curved up, away from the Word on gold-edged pages. I close my eyes and kiss, imagining the gold edges flinching under the spring rain beating the slanted window. And kiss, feeling Andre's big bottom lip between my lips.

We're naked, sitting on the passenger side of the front seat in his mom's Cutlass Supreme, windows steamed, rain playing the metal roof like a drum. My legs are tingling from straddling Andre for too long. I rise to my knees, reach back between the two front seats; Andre holds on to my ankles, and I stretch, take the Bible off the rear window's ledge, and hide it under the dry cleaning on the backseat, where countless nights between kisses I've prayed: *God, give me strength*. He pulls me back to him—calves, thighs, hips, waist—his hands sweaty against my bare skin, and holds me close for a while, his neck smelling like spring soap. I sniff his neck for a spot to kiss, like a dog looking for a spot to pee, and he tucks his long chin, giggles. It tickles. He reaches behind me, takes down the pink furry dice hanging from the rearview mirror, and holds them to my mouth. I blow, and he tosses them into the driver's seat. The pair of pink faces read seven: four and three. We kiss at our luck. He reaches for the long gold necklace still hanging from the rearview mirror. I reach for his hand and he leaves it: gold cross swinging.

Pressing into my scalp, he pushes my hair off my face and looks me in the eyes, wide open. We skip a few blinks. *Once I give it up, I can't claim it, can't wear it like a badge:* VIRGIN across my chest, off the tip of my tongue, between my praying hands. I place my hands on his chest, my light brown skin against his dark, and feel his heart—love beating fast as a tambourine on Sunday. Same love drumming up and between my thighs. He kisses my lips and I close my eyes: same sweet beat inside.

The sound of a thousand-pound bat cracking in the sky

makes me pull away from Andre, open my eyes, and see our naked bodies. Makes me want to run home with the rain sliding into me—baptizing me clean.

"What's wrong?" Andre asks, tilting his head to the side. "I thought we were going all the way this time."

I want to assure him that we are, but the fear of burning forever won't let me.

He bows his head, kisses my hand, and I feel his wet lips, soft on my skin. Another bow, and I see the raised, kidney-shaped birthmark on his shoulder I always trace with my tongue. His lips come back to my chin and I feel the heat between our hips, hear the rain spilling down from its bowl in the blue-black sky and beating the hood of the car. Another kiss, closer to my bottom lip, and I feel a space open between myself and the fear, like I am witnessing the fear outside of me, banging on the door, trying to get back in. Wet lips on my neck—it tingles—and I lower my chin, close my eyes, and dip back in.

After he tears open a silver square and slides on a condom, we come together. At first there is pain, but it goes away, obeying a deeper impulse, a swelling pleasure. I obey it, too, moving my body where it tells me—ten ways at once, all going under and under, itching for heat, for violence, beating its crazed wings at the root of my flesh, trying to break through, beating and plunging and beating and plunging and beating and squeezing his buckling bones, his suckling tongue, his hardening heart, beating him under and under.

Andre chokes my waist. Grunts. Freezes. Shakes. Lies back in the seat, eyes closed, at peace.

But I am still beating.

No song playing on the roof or in the car, we ride home with the windows down—cold, December wind whipping my face. I close my eyes to the blasts and try to pray. How dare I pray for forgiveness for something I want to do again? I open my eyes and look at Andre, who looks cool (his first time, too, but what do boys have to lose?), then down at the pink furry dice in his lap. Luck, huh? There's a chance we might die (people die in car accidents every day) and go to hell. Wouldn't be so lucky then. I take the necklace from the rearview mirror and slip it over my head—gold cross cold against my chest. My whole body goes cold, except for my left hand, held by Andre's right. He squeezes it at every stop sign and kisses it at every red light. I rub the gold cross all the way home and it finally warms.

At my front door, Andre asks for his mom's necklace. I want to keep it, sleep in it, wear it to church in the morning— be able to pray for grace in my pew with gold still warm on my chest. But I bow my head, and he reaches behind my neck, takes the chain, hangs it on his wrist, and hugs me close for a while, the cross beating my back.

He releases me and looks at his watch: 10:59. One more kiss, and I unlock the door, step inside—heat blasting. I want to run back outside, let Andre hold me longer, but I lock the door and set the alarm. Through mini blinds, I watch Andre return the Bible to the window ledge and hang the necklace on the rearview mirror: gold cross swinging in and out of the streetlight.

# S for . . .

**C**assie and I are in my room, making a list of all the boys we've ever liked or kissed or made out with. The door to my room is closed, and we're writing on the back side of it with chalk (Daddy coated my door with chalkboard paint after I saw the idea in *Seventeen* magazine). The top panel is Cassie's and reads:

Tommy—k
Brandon—k
Todd—k
Peter—l
John—k

Kevin—k

Ross—k

Luke—m

Most of the boys are from her old school, so I don't know them. But then she adds:

Justin—m

Mike—m

Charles—m

"Mike who?" I ask, sitting on my bed.

"Mike Murphy," she says, standing by the door. "I'm trying to think if I missed anyone," and she looks up and to the right.

"You didn't tell me about Mike!" I say. Mike is on the track team and he's our year. We see him all the time.

"There really wasn't much to tell," Cassie says. "He only gets an *m* by his name because I let him play with my right boob one time. It was weird. You remember that district track meet up in Conroe last year, when the boys and girls had to ride together."

"Yeah."

"Well, on the way back, he sat next to me by the window. I think you were asleep in the aisle seat across from me. Anyways, in the dark, he started playing with my right nipple.

I thought about making him stop, but it felt good, so I let him keep doing it until we got back to school."

"Then what?"

"That was it," Cassie says, and sits on my bed, her flannel pajama pant leg next to my flannel pajama pant leg. "We both acted like nothing ever happened. Your turn." She hands me the chalk.

I get up and write:

George–l
Mr. Franklin–l
Boy at mall–m
Andre–m

"How far have you and Andre gone?"

Because Andre goes to a different school, no one knows any of our business. "Basically everything but sex," I lie, and all my dormant guilt about having sex wakes up and runs to the center my chest. I sit down on the floor.

"Yeah, us, too," she says, talking about her and her boyfriend, Charles. She leans back against the wall and stretches her legs out on the bed.

"Can you believe Erica had sex with Kenan?"

I can, but I say, "No," trying to think like a virgin again.

Sometimes, I forget I'm having sex because no one at school or church knows. Forgetting makes me feel good . . . like God still loves me.

"And he's not even her boyfriend. She's such a ho."

*At least Andre's my boyfriend.* "I know, right."

"The whole school is talking about her. I bet her list couldn't even fit on the door." Cassie laughs.

*At least my list is short.* "On the walls," I add, and laugh, feeling better about myself.

Cassie laughs. "We would have to create a whole new category for her . . . *s* for *sex* . . . *s*'s all over the door and walls."

*Or s for sin*, I think, and the guilt in my chest balls up into a tight fist.

"Or *s* for *slut!*" She's cracking herself up.

The fist punches my insides and I say, "Or *s* for *stupid*, as in this conversation," to fight the guilt back.

Cassie's eyebrows fold in confusion.

"Or *s* for *snack*," I say, and stand up, trying to get rid of the weirdness in the room.

Cassie gets down from the bed. "Yeah, I'm kind of hungry, too . . . could use a *sandwich* or *something*," she says, and laughs.

But before we go to the kitchen to make two peanut butter and jelly sandwiches, I baptize the door with a wet washcloth. Wipe it clean.

# A Deep Conversation

*S*apience: *great wisdom and discernment. Sapience: great——.* Beside me in the library, a chair scrapes against the wooden floor, and I open my eyes and look over my shoulder. A tall, short-haired woman with a flat, oval face slides a leather bag out of the crook of her arm onto the long table with a thump. She smiles down at me. I return the smile but wonder why she wants to share elbow space when the rest of the table is empty.

She sits down and tilts the green glass lampshade, making its yellow light climb up my long arms. She takes out a book, removes the pencil that saved her place, and begins to read a poem called "Gospel."

I peek at the first two lines:

*Swing low so I*
*can step inside—*

*Focus, Taja.* I look down at my SAT flash card—*great wisdom and discernment*—but I can't remember the word on the back. I close my eyes and repeat "great wisdom and discernment" until *sapience* rises out of the darkness.

The woman circles *ship of voices* in her book, and I imagine the song of a hundred altos afloat on a sea.

I look to my next SAT flash card and read *ambrosial*. I flip the white three-by-five card over: *divinely sweet, fragrant, or delicious*. I close my eyes. *Ambrosial . . .*

The sound of pencil scratching paper makes me glance and see *blank with promise* inside another light-gray oval. I look ahead at the row of red leather-bound books, the chain of gold lettering across the tops of their spines, repeat, "ambrosial: divinely sweet, fragrant, or delicious," and slide the card to the bottom of the stack.

The woman gazes away from her book, past me, out the window, as if waiting for an answer to come from a faraway place, writes words with graceful loops and curves on the inside cover of her book, holds her pencil to her lips as if telling someone to shush, writes something else, and goes back to reading. I turn to see what she saw out of the window, but there are only the bare branches of a tall, skinny tree.

I look down at *vicissitude* on my top card, flip it over, read *a change, especially a complete change of condition or circumstances, as of fortune*, admiring the neat, backward-slanting letters of my own handwriting. I close my eyes. *Vicissitude: a change in fortune*. Beside me, a crisp page turns. Out of the corner of my eye, I watch the woman underline:

[. . . ] *But he slips*
*through God's net and swims*
*heavenward, warbling.*

I don't know what the words mean, but I wish I could read them aloud a thousand times. Alongside the verse, she scribbles a heart, and I regret not ever making such a mark in any of my books. Never again will I leave a margin empty beside a passage I love.

I try to switch to a new word, but a strange, warm feeling, swelling in my chest, paralyzes me: a hushed happiness, a deep pride, not for myself, for the woman beside me. A piece of me wants to bare it to her in a whisper, but more of me wants to claim it for myself, my future.

The sound of pencil on paper frees me. I look over at her circling "rows of deep green," move to my next card, which reads *extol*, and keep letting the words we hold say everything.

# Change Due

**F**ifty-fifty, fifty from him and fifty from me—that's how love is supposed to be. Fifty apiece, like each of us putting two quarters in a piggy bank and keeping two in our pockets, Washington's raised faces rubbing, his silver cheeks kissing. But Andre's love is greedy, trying to take three of my quarters, leaving me with only twenty-five cents.

No way. I need my fifty, my magic number: the number of steps I take from my room to the mailbox, where I look for application packets from my dream schools, the number of breaths I count in bed after I talk to God before my nightly walk through my wispy mind, the number of chapters in the book of the Bible farthest away from the flames of Revelations, the book where God turned fire into stars.

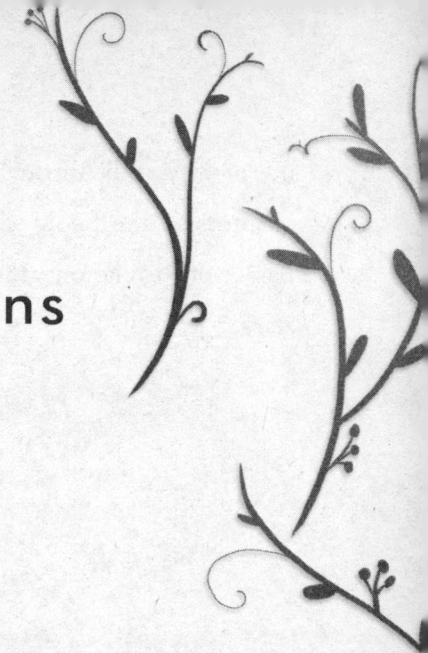

# Ghost Stains

**S**itting on stools at my kitchen counter, we write our names with Magic Markers on paper towels around tuna sandwiches and plain Lay's. "My signature is better," Andre says, and dots the *i* in his last name, green ink spreading.

"Believe that if you want to," I say, and take a sip of lemonade. Over the rim of my glass, I see Mom walk in.

"Thanks again for the sandwich, Mrs. Brown," Andre says, in his proper voice.

"Anytime," Mom says, her back toward us, sleeveless blouse baring her strong shoulders. She lifts the top off a big, black pot of beans on the stove; bay-leaf-scented ghosts rise and disappear into space. She stirs the simmering beans, giving more hazy figures a chance to escape. "Do me a favor and stir these beans about every ten minutes." She puts the lid back on. "And I don't know what y'all are doing over there, but don't stain my counters with those markers."

"We won't," I say.

She lowers her head as if looking at me over the top of invisible glasses. I lift the edges of the paper towels and let the four layers fall one by one, showing her we're protecting her faux wood. She nods and walks out, passing Naima on the way in.

"Oh, no he didn't," Naima says into the cordless phone, cradled between her shoulder and ear. "It's time to dismiss him." She looks at me without acknowledging Andre, gathers the corners of a paper towel with her chips and sandwich inside, and carries her bundle out of the kitchen. She doesn't like Andre. Says he walks with his arms away from his sides like they're scared of his body, either that or his body is scared of his arms; whatever the case, she doesn't know how I date someone so conflicted with themselves. "I wouldn't put up with that if I was you," she says in the hall and then quiets behind the door to her room.

I shake my head in annoyance, and Andre reaches over and writes his whole name in the top right corner of my paper towel. Crumbs pressing into my wrists, I write my name in red around the edge of one of his big chips, but only my first—the last will have to wait until I take another bite of my sandwich. As my lips touch the soft, white bread, Andre writes his last name beside my first—*Taja* and *Miller*, messy, but side by side in Christmas colors. I smile and roll my eyes. He flicks a few chips aside and writes more names below ours: James, Joy, Jalen, Jeremiah, Jasmine. "Our kids," he says, and eats one of his chips.

"Why do all their names have to begin with *J*?" I eat the last corner of my sandwich. Andre still has three whole bites left.

"They can all begin with *A* if you want, but *J* is right in the middle of *A* and *T*. I was trying to be fair," he says, chip crumb stuck to his greasy bottom lip. He licks it off.

"Fair? I know you're not talking about fair when you want to have five kids. You can't tell me I'd have time to write books and raise all of those kids." I eat my last chip, jealous of his sandwich staring at my lips.

"Dang, greedy girl." He holds his sandwich up to my mouth. "Say the magic word."

"Boy, please." I take a big bite.

"Okay, we'll have four. And I can help. They'll be Taja and *Andre's* kids. They'll have a daddy," he says, his nostrils growing open for more air.

"So exactly when do you think we're having all these kids?"

"Let me see . . . four years for us to graduate from UT—you up front with the nerds and me in the back with the cool people—a year to get married, and then another nine months. That's what? Six years." He stuffs the rest of his sandwich into his mouth.

*But what about my dream schools, the schools out of state— Stanford, NYU, Columbia, Yale—away, far away from everything I know, where there is space for mystery and mistakes,* I think, staring at the grease stains on my paper towels, eyes tracing their translucent shapes.

"Okay, I'll give you a break. Seven years." He goes after his last sip of lemonade—head back, clear cubes lying against his open mouth. A tiny stream trickles down and he shakes the glass, hurries the flow, and slurps until it's gone.

"Well, what if I get into Stanford or Yale or somewhere like that?" I say, looking over at him, feeling my eyebrows hike up as high as my tone.

"You know I can't get into any of those schools," he says, with the nerve to look at me with a straight face. "Half of them probably don't even have football teams."

"So?"

"What do you mean, 'So'? Don't you want to go to the same school?" he says, his thick eyebrows flexing.

"Yeah, but if Stanford says, 'Come on. You got in,' what do you want me to tell them? 'No'? I'd be crazy," I say, volume on my voice turned up.

"Okay, okay, relax. I don't even know why we're talking about this. Applications aren't due for another six months."

"Yeah, but I told you about Damon. I don't want the deadlines sneaking up on me."

"But schools like Stanford and Yale are almost impossible to get into anyway. What are the chances? Like one in fifty thousand applicants or something like that? We probably don't have anything to worry about," he says, and puts his hand on my thigh.

"You're right, *I* don't have anything to worry about," I say, stand up, and ball up my napkin. "I got a 1375 on my SATs and have a 4.67 GPA on a four-point scale, so that probably gives me a one-in-fifty chance right there." I pick up my glass and start walking around the counter into the kitchen. "Then you have to factor in my essay—and you know I can write—so that takes me down to one in ten." At the sink, I dump my lemonade and ice down the drain. "And don't forget about my extracurricular activities like student council, National Honor Society, and community service. Look at that, I'm down to one in five." I pull his napkin across the counter, closer to me, and eat one of his chips. "And you still haven't considered the fact that I'm nationally ranked in track. So that's one in two, a fifty-fifty chance." I ball up his napkin, chips crunching beside a future I know is not mine, and throw it in the trash.

"Oh, no! Look!" he says, licks his thumb, and rubs the countertop.

I step closer, see the green flecks, and fear freezes my neck, my jaw. I grab a scrubber and the spray cleaner from the cabinet under the sink, squeeze the trigger four times, and rub fast and hard. Faster. Harder. I stop and look: lighter but still there. A few more shots and I start scrubbing again.

"I got it," Andre says, adopting the job. After about a minute, he stops and we look, closer, look again, even closer, and again—there, a few faint green stains. Can't see them unless staring hard, but I spray again and he scrubs. When the stains are gone, I put the cleaner back under the sink, throw away the paper towels. But I don't go back and sit down.

"I'm sorry, baby. I know you can get into any school you want." Andre walks over to me. "I just can't imagine not being with you. I'd go crazy. I love you too much." He reaches for a hug, but I turn toward the stove, lift the top off the pot, and feel the steam climb over my mouth and nose, my face. Watch it curl, float, and fade.

*Attend me,*

*hold me in your muscular*

*flowering arms, protect me from*

*throwing any part of myself away.*

—Audre Lorde, *A Burst of Light*

# Sharp

**A**ndre is walking me to seventh period, holding my hand.

A group of his football teammates nod to him in passing. "Three p.m.!" one of them shouts.

Andre nods back and says, "Sharp."

"Three p.m.," Samantha says, walking past with her cheerleader friends.

"Sharp," Andre says again.

I swear I've heard *sharp* a million times today. Andre's planning a big senior prank at the pool after school. "To start the year off right," he keeps saying. Only three weeks since school began and already Andre has the whole school loving him. I guess I should be happy he's having such a good time fitting in . . . happy my social status has climbed a few notches just for being his girlfriend, but I'm not.

Andre swears his mom made him transfer to my school after receiving a letter over the summer saying his old school was installing metal detectors. But I think he transferred just to be closer to me. We already spend all weekend together and every day after school and sometimes early before school for a quick breakfast at IHOP. That's enough. Don't get me wrong, I love my boyfriend, but I need *some* space. Plus, I don't want everybody in our business.

At the door to my classroom, he kisses me good-bye and tells me he'll see me at the pool.

"But you know I don't swim," I say, still holding his hand.

"I won't let anything happen to you," he says, and lets go.

As he walks away, down the hall, I see LaToya approaching him.

"Three p.m.," she says.

And of course he says, "Sharp."

She walks past me, smiling, and I roll my eyes and walk into class.

Everyone's in bras and panties and boxer shorts, standing around the pool. Everyone except me. I'm standing in between Andre and Cassie, still fully clothed with the exception of my socks and boots.

"Come on," Andre says, "I have to start the countdown."

"Yeah," Cassie says. "Come on!" She's in a pink lace bra and panty set . . . went Victoria's Secret shopping for the occasion.

I stare at the blue water.

"Come on. I'll hold your hand," says Andre. "You'll be fine . . . the water isn't that deep."

"Okay," I whine, quickly take off my jean shorts and flannel shirt, and grab his right hand.

Andre raises his left hand to the ceiling and shouts, "Five . . . four . . . " His voice echoes in the large room.

The whole senior class joins in, "Three . . . "

I look down and scan the edges of the pool for the depth. Ten feet. *I'm not ten feet tall.*

"Two . . ."

*Why are we on the deep end? Of all the places to jump in.*

"One!"

I let go of Andre's hand and watch the room of barely covered bodies splash into the eight-lane pool. Free of my hand, Andre does a front flip in. People are swimming and laughing and giving high fives, but I'm still standing here in my Hanes.

*Jump, Taja, jump!* But my ten-year-old self, still standing on the edge of the diving board at the neighborhood pool, won't let me. *Jump!* I inch my toes forward on the wet white tiles, but she still refuses. So I grab my clothes and shoes and run into the girls' locker room, praying no one sees me.

In the locker room, I throw my boot at a long mirror. *Why couldn't you just jump in?* Hot, angry tears stream down my face. *I'm missing the biggest prank of the year.* I throw the second one harder, the mirror breaks, and small fragments fall to the floor. I stare at the hole, where the heel of my boot hit, at the lines radiating out of its center, at me in pieces. I want to lie down on the bench, but loud rap music starts flooding in from the pool. *I need to get out of here.* Teachers will be breaking up the party soon, and I'll be damned if I get a mark on my disciplinary record when I missed all the fun.

Walking to pick up my boots, I feel something sharp enter my foot. "Ouch!" I balance on my right leg and raise my left foot up to take a look. A tiny piece of glass is lodged under my skin, only its sharp edge sticking out. I try to grab it, but I can't. Try again with the tips of my fingernails . . . still can't. *I don't have time for this,* I think, grab my boots, get dressed, sneak out of the other door into the gym, and limp to my car, where Naima's standing around with her friends.

"Why aren't you at the pool?" she calls out as I approach. "And why are you limping?"

"How do you know about that?" I say.

"The whole school knows."

"Let's go," I say, and unlock the doors to my Corolla.

"So lame." She rolls her eyes. "I guess I'll see y'all Monday," she says to her friends and gets in.

Baskin-Robbins on the way home  Naima begs and I make her get out and pay. Licking the cold, butter-pecan sweetness in the waffle cone almost makes me forget about the broken piece of glass stuck in my left foot . . . about being afraid to jump.

When we walk into the house, Mom immediately calls my name.

"Yeah," I say.

"Oh, good," she says to someone else, in a lowered voice. "She's home. I knew she wouldn't be involved in that mess."

I head straight to my room.

"Let me call you back," she says.

When I get to my room, I sit on my bed to take the pressure off my foot.

"Knock knock," Mom says as she opens the door. She walks in and stands beside my bed. "Heard about the whole pool thing at school."

"Yeah?" I say, and slide my shoe off, keeping my socks on and the sole of my foot facing the floor in case there's blood.

"I'm proud of you," she says, and places her hand on my back.

"Thanks," I say, hoping she'll leave.

"The school is holding all the seniors in the auditorium. Calling everyone's parents. There's talk of suspensions."

"Really?" I say, glad I don't have to deal with all that.

"That was Andre's mom on the phone."

*Since when did you start talking to Andre's mom?*

"She's furious. The principal is saying Andre was the ringleader. She's going to ground him for a month."

*A month!* A sharp pain pierces my chest, worse than the pain in my foot. I feel like I've just been grounded, too. *I can't make it a month without seeing Andre.* Tears start rising up until I remember he goes to my school.

"If Cassie was involved, I'm sure she'll be grounded, too. You didn't know about any of this?"

"No," I lie, and pick up *Harry Potter and the Sorcerer's Stone* off my nightstand. It's wrapped with a paper grocery sack like all my schoolbooks so she won't know I'm reading it. When *Harry Potter* first came out, she said she didn't want me reading anything about magic.

"Hmph. Well, if you ever hear of something like this happening in the future, you need to tell someone."

*Yeah, right.* "Okay, Mom," I say, and open the book.

"Well, okay then." She leaves and closes the door behind her.

I put down the book, take off my sock, and look at the bottom of my foot. No glass, only a circle of pink skin. I swipe the circle with the palm of my hand. No sharp edge. I press it—tender!—and feel a lump. Squeeze it, sucking air in between my teeth, but nothing comes out, not even blood. Keep squeezing . . . nothing . . . harder . . . nothing.

Loose laces, thick socks, and a slight limp until I forget about the little broken piece inside of me.

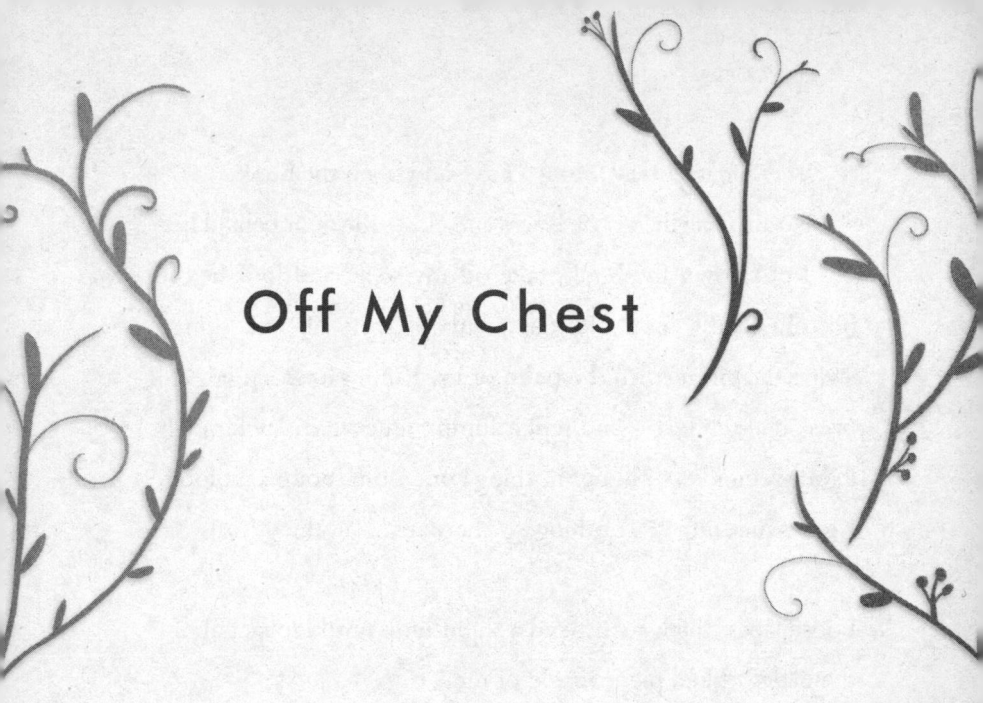

# Off My Chest

I'm at the post office, standing at the front of the line, holding my completed college applications, and my right foot won't stop tapping. *Stop* and it soon forgets and starts tapping again. *Stop* and it keeps tapping. *Stop* but it won't listen. I look up at a poster with *In God We Trust* printed over an American flag, bring the words *God* and *trust* into my chest, and my foot rests.

Then the lights go out. Everything around me is black. And quiet. No envelopes sliding or receipts printing or boxes tumbling or chatter or coughs. *What just happened?* It feels like the end of the world. Pastor Hayes always says the rapture can happen any time and any place. *But now? Could this be my punishment for having sex? Jesus coming back on one of the most important days of my life and leaving me to burn in hell?* My eyes swell with tears and I clutch the seven large envelopes to my chest. *How could you?*

"Looks like someone forgot to pay the bills," a man in line behind me says.

Dead silence. At least one person in line should've laughed. *He's left behind, too.* Sweat slides down my right temple off the side of my cheek. It's a cold January day, but it's hot as hell in here. *Oh, no . . . hell is on its way.*

I close my eyes, press my head against the stack of envelopes, and try to pray. But I'm mad and this comes out instead: *I follow all of Your rules . . . do everything right . . . everything but have sex. Are You really going to punish me this much just for having sex? Give me a break!*

It heats up ten degrees and I sweat harder.

*I'm sorry for talking to You like that. I don't know what I was thinking. Please forgive me. I won't have sex anymore. I promise. Just forgive me and take me. Please, God. Don't leave me here to burn in hell.*

A man behind the counter says, "Hold on, folks. We should have the power back on in a sec."

I let out a deep breath, open my eyes to darkness, and

wipe my tears with my shoulders, wool coat scratching my face. *Thank God.*

The lights power on and people clap.

But I look down at my applications and they have wrinkles on the sides where I've clutched them too tight. And the top one, my Stanford application, my first choice, has a dark oval from my sweaty forehead. I start crying all over again.

"Next," says a post office lady in red glasses.

I walk up to the counter and try to press down the edges of my envelopes against the hard surface.

"Ah, poor baby . . . look at you. You must've been scared to death."

I stop pressing, look up at her, and say, "They need to be perfect," not caring that I'm crying to a complete stranger. Then, as fast as I can, I start waving my hand back and forth over the wet mark.

"Let me see what you got there," she says, and slides the envelopes away from me. "Oh, your college applications. Now I see . . . my daughter's a sophomore at Tulane. I remember her going through this."

"They need to be perfect," I say again, crying harder.

"But they're fine," she says. "This is what has you so upset?" She points to the wet mark. "Oh, honey, it'll dry."

"And . . . and," I say, and point to the wrinkles.

"The little creases are nothing. Mail gets bent and creased all the time."

"But they need to be perfect," I plead.

The lady lowers her head and looks at me over the top of her red glasses. "Nothing or no one is perfect, child," she says with a you'd-better-listen-to-me voice and face. She lowers her head even more and her messy top bun plops forward. "You're just going to have to trust you did the best you could and send these applications here on their way."

I grab the word *trust*, pull it inside me, and stop crying.

She takes the Stanford envelope and places it on a silver scale.

I wipe my face with the back of my hand.

She weighs the other six. "That'll be two dollars and ten cents."

As I reach for my wallet, she stamps the Stanford envelope in the upper right-hand corner and tosses it in a large, canvas mail cart. When it disappears, I feel lighter. Another stamp and another envelope is on its way to a school of my choice. Even lighter. Another envelope is out of my sight. And lighter. No more essay writing. Lighter. No more proofreading. Lighter. No more asking for recommendations. Lighter. No more double-checking and triple-checking the checklist. Light.

# I Can't

"Stop it," I say, and pull up my pink Victoria's Secret panties.

"Come on," Andre says. "Not even on Valentine's Day?" He starts sliding them down again. We're lying on top of his bed, facing each other in our underwear. His mom is on a date.

"I'm serious, Andre," I tell him, and pull them back up.

Andre kisses my mouth with his thick, soft lips and slides his hand between my legs. "Are you sure you don't want me to take them off?" He slowly glides his hand back and forth.

Pulses of pleasure, and before saying, "Yes, I'm sure," I get one more kiss.

"Come on . . . it's been over a month. I'm gonna get blue balls," he whines, and pokes out his bottom lip.

I gently bite it.

"Just the tip." He kisses my neck.

Tingles upon tingles upon tingles. "I wish I could but I can't."

"What do you mean you can't? I don't get it!" Andre says, and rolls away from me toward the window. His squeaking bed sounds just as mad as him.

"I told you," I say, and place my hand on his smooth, brown back. "I can't take the guilt anymore."

"We've been having sex for over a year and all of a sudden you decide to feel guilty? I'm telling you right now . . . I'm not gonna be able to deal with this too much longer."

I lay my head in the dip in his back. "I've always felt guilty," I explain, and just like that, guilt rises up and takes a seat on my chest. "I've tried my best not to, but I can't," I say, my voice cracking under the weight. "And I can't take it anymore." Tears rush behind my eyes and stream down my face, pooling where my cheek and Andre's back meet.

Andre turns around and puts his arms around me. "Don't cry."

My body shakes in his arms. "I'm sorry, but . . . but . . . I just—"

"Shh," he says, and holds me tighter. "It's okay."

But lying there, feeling Andre's chest against my chest, feeling his bulge against my leg, I can't get his words—*I'm not going to be able to deal with this*—out of my head. He squeezes me tighter and I try . . . rubs my back and I try . . . kisses my forehead and I try.

# Delivery

Cramped in the mailbox between catalogs, circulars, and standard-sized envelopes is a fat white packet. A fat white packet!—exactly what people say to look for . . . exactly what I've been praying for the past few months. I rescue it, pulling it away from the others, and cradle its weight in my palms. Its back flap greets me, baring the crimson seal of a tall pine. I know it, want to kiss it, flip the packet over to be sure. Yes! There, in the top left corner: *Stanford*. I press the red letters to my chest and feel crushed under their weight, their promise, which is spreading, numbing my legs.

I kneel in the wet grass with *Stanford* face down on my

thighs. The white packet now seems like a stranger. For all I know, it could have a rejection inside. I look up at the sun, hanging low in the sky, just over the tallest pine, and pray, *Please, God*.

I poke my thumb into the gap under the closing flap, tear the packet open, and pull out a stack of papers. My eyes go as far as the first word, *Congratulations!* It fills me. I stop reading, start screaming. My voice is ringing, carrying me away to a new corner of my expanding world. I cross into California and melt into it, its golden sweetness, and feel it saving my place, awaiting my delivery.

# Trying to Tell
# You Something

As I rock heels to tiptoes, reading my acceptance letter to Andre over the phone, my voice high, expanding each long vowel, I notice sounds coming through my receiver—a series of hard, brisk letter *B*'s *and P*'s, followed by *S*'s, and *T*'s, making a simple beat.

I stop reading, lower my heels, and ask, "Are you listening?"

"Yeah," he says, and begins a new beat, a rapid series of *B*'s that sounds like he's spitting out something nasty.

"How can you be listening when you're beatboxing?" I touch *Congratulations*—safe behind the glass of my favorite gold frame, the one Daddy made last, carving a butterfly in every corner.

"You act like I can't do two things at once. I hear you," he says, his tone spiked in annoyance.

"Even if you *can* hear me, it's still rude."

"Look, if you're going to read the letter, then hurry up and read it. I don't have all day," he says, and lies down. I can hear his bed squeaking as his long body settles.

Something tells me to hang up the phone in his face, but I choose not to listen. I have a plan, a careful plan, and I want to see it through. All I need to do is finish reading the letter, allowing him to hear how excited I am, but then tell him that I don't think I should go, breathing loudly and unevenly, saying that I can't possibly be so far away from him, sniffling and cracking my voice, that I love him and can't live without him. I know then he'll ask me if I've gone crazy and tell me that I must go, that he loves me and won't have it any other way.

"Fine," I say, rejuvenated by my plan's promise. I run my pinky finger through the grooves of the hindwing in the top right corner of the frame. "Should you choose to enroll at Stanford, you will meet and study with some of the most elite faculty and students in the world."

The *b* word, *titties*, *Big Poppa*—snatches of a rap song mixed with pounding sounds. He's turned up the volume on his stereo and is knocking on his headboard. I imagine him lying on his back, long legs spread wide, knuckles and wrists taking turns banging on his black lacquered bed—blurring the words of "The Dream Keeper" in the oval frame I'm staring at.

"Hello," he says.

I want to ask him to please turn the music down, explain the letter is special to me, but something tells me he isn't stupid and refuses to let me speak.

"Hello," he says, louder, harder.

I know his thick eyebrows are folding in on themselves. I want them to stop, want to keep my plan alive. I part my lips to say something to calm him down, but only air comes out.

"Oh, so you're ignoring me, now? You're calling yourself mad, now? Well, I'm sorry I didn't hold my breath while you were reading your precious letter. You act like you want me to sit up here with my lips sealed and my hands folded in my lap like I'm in kindergarten or something. Like you're the president or something. You must think you're reading the Declaration of Independence or something. It's just an acceptance letter. You already have seven. What's one more? You act like getting into Stanford is all that."

"Well, *excuse* me for being excited about getting into one of the best schools in the country, no, in the world.

Maybe if you had been listening, you would know Stanford has more than eighty majors and minors, including creative writing. I can take a class where the only homework I ever have is to read and write poetry. Can you imagine? Not to mention their study-abroad programs. I can spend a semester in Italy, Africa, Spain, or France. Can you imagine? Oh, my bad, I almost forgot—*you* have nothing to do with *all that*." I hang up.

My head and heart are pounding . . . my throat is sore . . . my legs don't feel like they can hold me up, so I kneel down on the carpeted floor. *That was not how I planned it.* I look up at Andre in a square frame, sitting on a swing in the park, and feel a hot, tingling knot at the back of my throat. *That was not the way it was supposed to go.* I release the Hang Up button and use both thumbs to dial Andre's number. It rings and rings, six long times, and then he picks up. No, it's his mom's recorded voice. The knot turns to tears, real and uncontrollable. I hang up and press Redial. It rings once: *Please pick up.* Twice: *Please, I need to talk to you.* Three times: *You know going to Stanford is my dream.* Four times: *But we can still be together.* Five: *Write letters and talk once a week.* Six: *Get married and have five kids.* Answering machine. I wipe the snot off my top lip with the back of my hand, hang up, and press Redial. One ring and he answers! *Click*, and then a dial tone—loud and clear.

# Revelations

"Cassie, you better stop lying."

"I'm not lying," she tells me through the phone.

"Andre did not say that. Andre did not tell everyone that," I say, sitting on my bedroom floor, back against my bed.

"Yes, he did. Well, he told Joe and Brandon, and you know how they like to talk. They said y'all have been having sex for, like, over a year. If you had sex, just say you had sex, Taja. It's not a big deal."

"But I didn't," I say, tugging at a chunk of beige carpet.

"Swear to God you didn't."

"That's blasphemy."

"Well, cross your heart and hope to die."

"I'm not twelve."

"Well, prove to me you're not lying."

"I don't have to prove anything to you. I don't care if you believe me or not. I know what I am. I'm a good girl. I sing in the church choir. I keep my eyes closed during the whole prayer, even when my daddy's praying and that's at least fifteen minutes. I take sermon notes. And when the pastor calls out a scripture, I find it quick because I know the books of the Bible: front to back and back to front. Ask me what comes after Mark—no, too easy. Before Samuel, Isaiah, or Song of Songs—oh, that's right, you can't test me on what you don't know. Name anything that comes before Revelations. Do you know what happens in Revelations, Cassie? Hell happens in Revelations. And once you go, you can't escape."

"Oh, hell. I forgot. The place souls burn forever," she says, sarcastically.

"Yes, hell!" and I tug harder.

"And how exactly does a soul burn?"

"I don't know. I can't ask questions like that in Sunday school. Even if I did, they'd just think I was crazy. My soul burns now . . . I'm losing my mind. I know they don't have an answer for that."

"You're not crazy, Taja. You just need to stop lying to

yourself . . . and to me . . . and to everybody. Forget about all this hell business. It's nonsense."

"Nonsense? I pray for you, Cassie. I pray you get saved and don't go to hell."

"Don't worry, I won't, because I don't believe in hell."

"Well, you should."

"Why? So I can be like you? Lying and acting crazy?"

"You're the one who's lying. You're probably just jealous of Andre and I. Wish you and Charles came close to what we have." I yank out two threads of carpet and place them on my bare thigh.

"Fuck you, Taja."

"*F* me? Forget you, too."

"Oh, you can't say *fuck*?"

"No, I won't say the *f* word. I'm not like you, Cassie. I don't swear. Ladies don't swear. Or give it up before we get married. My daddy says nobody wants to marry used goods. He says it's like going grocery shopping and realizing someone has already taken a bite out of your candy bar, a sip of your milk, a strip of your bacon. When you get to the cash register, would you want to pay? My brother says he wouldn't pay. Do I look like used goods to you? I don't think so," I say, and flick the threads off my leg.

"Just tell the truth already!" she screams.

"What? You still think I'm lying? Why would I lie?" I yell, and hang up.

# The Price
# of Admission

Lying in bed, staring at the slit of yellow light under my door, I see a shadow and hear the click of my latch leaving its hole. My door swings open. Naima stands in the brightness of the hall. *She knows.* We don't share secrets but the whole school knows.

She walks in and my room fades back to black as she closes the door behind her. I want to scream, "Get out of my room," but instead I close my eyes and pretend to be asleep.

Her footsteps fall silent upon the carpet, but I can feel her coming toward me. Judging me. Pitying me. Blaming me for being stupid enough to love him. *I hate her.*

"Taja," she whispers.

I keep pretending.

"Taja."

On my back, I lie perfectly still and pray she goes away.

"I brought you one of my CDs."

"Huh," I say, trying to sound sleepy, hoping it's *Destiny's Child*. I left mine in Andre's car.

"It's the *Waiting to Exhale* soundtrack," she says. "It always helps me after breakups."

*Helps you with what? You're always the one doing the breaking up.* I hear the CD's plastic case slide across my nightstand and say, "Thanks."

"Scoot over." She lifts her leg onto my bed, her rough sole rubbing against my shin under the covers. I slide toward the wall and let her in. We haven't laid in bed together since we shared a room, but somehow the darkness makes me feel like it was only yesterday.

Naima drapes her leg over mine. I free mine from underneath and drape mine over hers. Hers over mine. Mine. Hers. It's the game we used to play.

"So, is it true?" she asks.

The directness of her question stuns me and I lose my tongue.

"Well?"

My secret fumbles about for a place to hide, but even in the dark, there is nowhere.

Naima takes her leg off mine.

*Don't leave me.* I fill my lungs from bottom to top and push out, "Yes," feeling some of the horror of the truth, the shame, release, too.

"I knew it!" Naima says, and puts her leg back on mine. "How did it feel? Did it hurt?"

"Um, yeah, a little," I say, surprised by the delight in her voice. "But only when it first starts. After it gets going, it feels . . . kind of . . . good." *I can't believe I'm telling her all this.*

"I thought I would do it with Derrick one day. I just knew I loved him. But then I saw him use the nail of his pinky finger to pick out a piece of pepperoni stuck between his front two teeth and I changed my mind."

"But you pick your teeth all the time."

"True. Maybe it was the way he picked them. Who knows? All I know is after that, I knew he wasn't the one."

"I thought Andre was the one, but I guess I was wrong," I say, hoping my sadness doesn't make its way to her under the covers.

"Hate to say I told you so, but—"

"Would you shut up," I say, free my right leg from Naima's weight, and bring it to meet my left.

"I don't know why you're getting mad at me. I'm not the one going around school telling everybody your business."

I search my mind for a comeback, but all I can hear is, *telling everybody your business*—a soft, numbing echo. "Just get out."

"With pleasure." She climbs out of my bed, takes her CD, and leaves, slamming the door behind her.

The yellow slit under my door turns black.

*I hate her. I should've never told her. I should've lied.*

But lying in bed, with only blackness to stare at, the truth feels different inside me, like it's a part of me, like I own it, and I change my mind. Telling the truth was worth it.

# Almost
# Everything

Underneath the bleachers, hiding from the sun, I wait to lose my last jump. Lying on my back with my head resting on my track bag, I watch bits of blue sky peek through steel strips. On the other side, whistles blow. People cheer, shout, and clap. The *click-clack* of shoes climb up, down, and across the stairs. A couple times, loose change escapes pockets above me and rains down, but I don't reach out my arms or hands.

"Get up!" Cassie says, nudging my left shoulder with the toe of her cleat. She's standing over me.

"I can see up your nose," I say.

"I'm not playing, Taja. Get up."

A drop of sweat slides off the tip of her small round nose, and I quickly shift out of its way and sit up.

"The triple jump is in less than twenty minutes. You should have *been* warming up," she says, sweating, her light-brown skin glowing red.

"Here I come," I say, and stand up, noticing a nasty taste in my mouth, same as after a nap. "But first, I need some gum."

"Gum? Are you serious?" She claps her hands so close to my face I can feel the air race up the slant of my cheeks. "Hello! This is the district track meet, Taja! Our senior year! Must I remind you that you didn't even place in the long or high jump? And for what? Andre is still stupid and y'all are still broken up. Now, the triple has always been yours. You can't let him take it. Forget him and come on."

I know Cassie means well, but I don't know how to feel about her being all up in my face—eyebrows buckled, left side of her upper lip hiked up. She sounds like Mom, but she isn't. "Didn't I say I was coming?"

She walks off with her weight on her heels to keep the spikes of her cleats from biting the concrete.

I grab my bag, sling my cleats, tied together by their strings, over my right shoulder, and walk to the concession stand—Juicy Fruit calling my name.

The concession stand, a red-roofed shack with a large

rectangular window, backs up to the chain-link fence near the stadium's entrance. On the counter, inside a big glass box, popcorn bubbles over the sides of a suspended metal pot. It smells burnt. I measure the two lines. The right one stretches three bodies past the left. But the left has more groups and pairs, standing side by side, which can take more time. I notice a pair at the front of the left line. A tall boy biting a pickle, accepting bills from the cashier. He turns to put his change in his front pocket. Andre. The girl standing beside him bites his pickle. A girl with the backs of LaToya's hairy legs coming out of green track shorts, a girl with LaToya's stacks in her hair. Andre bites the pickle again and looks up, dead at me. Then he kisses her, tongue and everything.

A bell should have rung to signal the start of a fight before Andre pounded a hole through my chest, knocked hope right out of my mind. But nothing warned me of the beating waiting around the corner. I can't breathe. Can't blink. Can't move. Can't believe. *You're not kissing LaToya. You wouldn't. You're not.* But he is. *How could you?* Right here for me to see. *This is me. Don't you still love me?* After he pulls his lips from hers, he looks at me again—brown eyes cold, like we had never been—and takes another bite. *No, Taja. Come on.* And before LaToya can turn, see me, and get her blows in, I take off running toward the field, tongue still covered with a bitter film.

I cross the red clay track, eight lanes divided by bright white lines. *It's over*. Before the kiss, I prayed Andre would come to his senses and we'd make up. *It's really over*. I stop running. It's hard to see through the blur of my tears, through the dizzying colors of track uniforms zipping this way and that across the field. *And of all people, LaToya!* I look up at the clear turquoise sky in search of relief and feel my tears slip beneath my temples, form tiny pools inside my ears. The sky makes me feel small, stupid for loving Andre. *I'm over here crying and losing jumps, and he's over there with his tongue down LaToya's throat.* I wipe my face, put on my cleats, and run across the field to the landing pit, spikes biting the earth.

The judge has already raked the sand. It's too late for practice jumps, for placing markers so my feet will know where to land. Pieces of different-colored tape line the side of the runway. Cassie practices in the grass—each hop, step, and jump in line with her green tape. She sees my face, stops, walks over, and asks, "You okay?"

"Yeah," I say. "Tell you about it later. Go ahead and keep practicing." She's being such a good friend, and I don't want my drama interfering with her jump any more than it has already.

Cassie looks at the raked pit and says, "You can practice with me if you want."

Even though we're the same height, I know her marks won't

be mine, but I don't care. I just want to jump, feel the air under my legs, feel something else. At first, I try to hit her marks, but nothing—the swing of my arms, the lift of my legs—seems right. So I stop thinking about the marks, the individual parts, and start feeling the whole movement of the jump. And just when I start to sense a rhythm, the judge blows the whistle for the girl from Klein Oak to make her first attempt.

Cassie and I stop and watch, and Andre climbs back into the ring inside my head. *And the nerve to share a pickle with her! That was our thing. Is nothing we did sacred? Nothing we shared? You liar! You told me you loved me. You thief! You took everything I had to give.*

I placed eighth in the preliminaries, so I have to jump last, look on at seven girls sprint, lift off, and glide, while fighting Andre in my mind. When the judge finally blows his whistle and nods his white visor at me, Cassie is in the lead with a jump of thirty-nine and three-quarters feet.

I scratch my first two tries—toe of my cleat over the white take-off board. Then, with Cassie clapping off to the side, I tell myself, *This is mine*. And without measuring my steps, I run down the runway, lose my thoughts somewhere in the speed of my legs, catch a rhythm—hop, step, jump—and take off flying through the air. My thoughts are waiting for me in the dirt, where I land after my long flight, but by then I've already won.

# Life After Death

Tell me again how to go inside. How to close my eyes and feel tiny dots and tingles. I used to feel them all the time. They used to remind me I was alive. I wonder if you can see them—wherever you are—billions of suns spinning beneath the wrinkles of your skin. Or maybe you have smooth skin, and you're that little girl with two long braids again. Or maybe you have no skin, and light flows into you and out of you like waves. Or maybe just maybe you're a big fish with silver lips and shimmering turquoise scales.

Tell me again and again about God. About how He's for everyone but still mine. It's like the time Daddy played his saxophone for the whole congregation, waxy notes of praise rising and floating like your pipe's smoke, but it felt like we were on the back deck, underneath the blue-black sky, and he was playing for me, alone. Maybe you were listening.

Explain again how to feel the energy of our ancestors in my hands so I can feel you, and your power can help pull the purple out of these bruises that have numbed me. Again and again, please say the words that will open me up, dissolve the dead parts, clear out space for gold notes to dance, shuffling their feet and flapping their elbows, and remind me how to love life.

*Freeing yourself was one thing;*

*claiming ownership of that freed self was another.*

—Toni Morrison, *Beloved*

# The Deep Blue

Each time Daddy puffs his tobacco pipe, chocolate smoke rises from his mouth, curls out of his cracked car window, and disappears into the dark blue morning. Despite the disappearance, the inside of his car is hazy and gray and sweet—I breath it in deep.

We're on I-45, driving to Galveston. Just Dad and me. Mom didn't want to miss her deaconess duties of distributing Holy Communion in her white dress. And Naima didn't feel like waking up before the sun.

"Thanks again for coming with me," Daddy says, and takes a puff. "I like getting out over the water sometimes. It clears my mind." He glances over at me, almost fully reclined in the passenger seat, and takes another puff. "Makes me forget about everything."

I sense he's searching for more ways to talk around my sadness. "You know, Mom says smoking can kill you," I say, trying to keep my sadness out of reach.

"Well," and another puff. Then he takes the pipe in his left hand, flips on his left signal light, and gets over to create an empty lane between us and a sixteen-wheeler. "I guess there's a risk," he says, speeding up to pass the giant truck, "but Gigi smoked a pipe all her life and she was fine."

"Fine? She died of cancer!" I immediately regret the way my words come out. "Sorry, I didn't mean it like that. I just mean——"

"It's okay. Gigi lived a long time. Some kind of disease is eventually going to get everybody. That's just life." He stares at the road ahead, pipe still in his left hand.

I shift my body in the seat and curl up on my side, facing Daddy. I'm getting sleepy and want to close my eyes, but his last statement is bothering me. "Plenty of people die of natural causes. Maybe Gigi could've lived longer if she didn't smoke."

"Yeah, maybe," he says, and doesn't take a puff.

Again I shift in my seat, trying to make myself comfortable

enough to fall asleep. The seat belt cuts across my neck, and I pull it down, underneath my arm.

Daddy's round eyes meet mine squarely, like he's about to tell me to sit straight in the seat and put my seat belt on correctly, but he doesn't. "But maybe not," he picks up where he left off. "Life is full of risks, Taja. Your mom and I have always tried to shield you from those risks, but you'll be living on your own soon . . . making your own decisions . . . deciding for yourself what's worth the risk."

Holding the steering wheel steady with one knee, Daddy grabs his silver lighter from the center console, flicks on the flame, and makes fiery circles around the pipe's bowl until sweet smoke is rising from his mouth again.

The thud of the trunk slamming shut wakes me up and I open my eyes. *We're here.* It's usually dark when we get to Galveston, but the sun is already bright in the sky.

Stepping out of the car, the smell of salt and fish fills my nostrils. I open the back door to get my rod and chair. No need for nets, rope, and chicken necks. Daddy doesn't like to crab.

"I already got everything," Daddy says, loosening the chin cord on his fishing hat. He's standing behind the car. "Carried it down when you were asleep," and he starts toward the pier, carrying only a tackle box.

"Thanks," I say, and follow, sun already warm on my skin.

"Looks like we have the pier all to ourselves today. Probably because of this heat. The weatherman promised it would be cooler. Sorry, we don't have to stay long."

"It's okay," I say, feeling something rising up inside me, making my legs move faster, toward the pier. Walking ahead of Daddy, I try to grab it and figure out what it is. But it's making too many movements—swinging, plunging, kicking, and flying—fleeing me.

When I take my first step onto the wooden planks of the pier, the memory of a crab escaping Mom's cooler, scooting down the pier, and leaping into the ocean—free—climbs to the front of my mind. And suddenly the pier, stretched out to meet the sky and sea, feels like the most important invitation I've ever received. I take off running and when I get to the pier's end, I kick off my shoes and quickly climb onto the wooden rails. My long toes grip the railing for a second, loosen, and let go.

Falling feels like an eternity.

Falling feels wild and bright and fully alive.

But when my body hits the water, the little breath I have left over from the run rushes out of my lungs. I try to take another breath, but I'm a second too late and my throat fills with water. I panic and flail my arms hysterically, choking and gasping for air. I go up and down and up and down and up and down until my limbs grow tired.

Then I just go down, bubbles tinkling in my ears and nose. Down, terrified of the swelling darkness around me. Down. *All I wanted to do was feel free. But this water doesn't feel free. It's swallowing me whole.* Down. *Are you really about to let yourself die down here?* Down. But darkness is all around me, locking me up. *You better find a way out!* I look up and see light—sharp, bright rays piercing the deep blue. *Come on, Taja.* I raise my arms and push the water down. Raise my arms and push the water down. *Go, Taja, go.* Raise and push and raise and push until my head is above water.

"Taja! Taja!" screams Daddy.

I cough and cough and gasp for air.

"Taja!" Daddy screams again.

More air.

Daddy's arms are around my shoulders, pulling me.

"You okay?" he asks, panting.

More air, chest pounding.

"You okay?" he repeats.

More air, waves splashing my chin. I look at the pier. *I did it.*

"Taja?" he says louder.

"Yes, I'm okay," I finally have the breath to say. I relax and let Daddy pull me, each breath feeling less and less forced. Let Daddy pull me until I'm breathing with ease. But before we get to the shore, I tap his arm and say, "Let go."

He holds on tighter.

I tap his arm again. "I can swim the rest of the way."

"No," he says, still holding on.

"Yes," and I push his arm.

He lets go and I float on my back, kick my feet, reach my arms open, and pull them down toward my sides. Reach and pull and reach and pull, looking up at the bright blue sky.

As soon as we're out of the water, Daddy says, "What were you thinking?"

"It wasn't about thinking," I say, bent over, hands on my knees, trying to catch my breath.

"Clearly," and Daddy flops down and lies back in the sand.

Dripping with water, I defend myself, "It's something I've wanted to do for a long time." Then I tug at my wet jean shorts, which are suctioning everything from waist to knee. "I'd forgotten. But today I remembered."

"You could've died, Taja."

"No . . . well, maybe . . . but I didn't. I wouldn't have let myself," I say, and lie down beside Daddy, the responsibility for my own life rattling around inside me like a pop-top lid inside an empty soda can.

"You can't control everything, Taja," Daddy says in a soft voice, eyes closed to the sun.

"I know, Daddy. But I can control a lot." The rattling stops and responsibility sinks in.

Daddy nods and three seagulls in the air above me squawk and flap their white wings. The tall crest of a wave curls and crashes, and white foam runs up high to kiss my feet. And I can't stop grinning . . . at what feels like a celebration for me.

# So Much
# Promise

**O**ops! And down goes a dancing boy's plastic cup into the grass. "Sorry!" and I whiz past him to kick the glittery balloon back into the air. If it touches the ground, I'm out.

"Time's up!" Naima shouts over music playing from Damon's huge speakers. "If you take this long to get to first base, then you're automatically out." We're in the backyard, at my graduation party, playing kickball with balloons—a good way to avoid taking pictures and receiving praise all night. It's Keisha, Cassie, and me against Naima and two of her friends.

"You can't just make up rules like that," I snap back.

Another kick and glitter swirls around inside the clear balloon. A few pieces briefly light up, like the fireflies blinking around everybody's legs in the dark—feels like magic. I gaze upon the glitter, willing it to go toward first base, but the balloon decides to drift toward the fence, where two girls from down the street are playing a hand-clapping game, singing:

> "*Shimmy, shimmy cocoa pop*
> *Shimmy, shimmy boom.*"

The balloon hits the girls' fingertips and bounces up toward a string of silver lights. "No!" I plead. If the balloon pops on the hot lights, I'm out. I reach out to rescue it with my hands but stop myself.

"Damn, that would've been good!" Naima says, as if no church people are around.

"I'm not that stupid," I reply, and the balloon turns against the ceiling of strung lights and heads back down. But my eyes keep climbing past the lights, right up to the crescent moon. *Moonie*—Andre's nickname, and my mind begins a playback of us grabbing each other's long chins. "When are they supposed to get here?" I ask Cassie. Her boyfriend is bringing his cousin with him to the party. And Cassie says he's *fwine*, as in finer than fine.

"I don't know. Charles said they'd be here . . . probably just running late," Cassie answers.

When the balloon finally comes down, I kick it carefully to avoid the half dozen polyester pant legs of the men who play with Daddy in the saxophone quartet at church. "Excuse me," I say, giving them a smile, and the balloon finally moves toward first base: the back side of the table holding my presents and cake. I kick it again and I'm one yard closer to the *Congratulations*-patterned tablecloth, hanging down over the deck's wooden planks. Again and—

"It's time to cut the cake," Mom says, and grabs the balloon.

"Boom, you're out!" Naima shouts. Her friends start cheering.

"No, that was interference," I yell.

"Yeah!" Keisha backs me up.

Mom turns toward Naima and says, "Go tell Damon to turn the music down."

"Okay, but you're still out, Taja!" Naima declares. She takes off and almost runs into Ms. Carter from across the street.

"Come on," Mom says, and tugs down on my new jean skirt. It's the third time she's done it tonight, her way of letting me know she thinks it's too short.

"Mom," I moan, take back the balloon, and follow her to the patio.

* * *

"We just want to thank everyone for coming out to celebrate Taja tonight," Mom starts.

I'm standing between her and Daddy, in front of the gifts and cake, holding on to the balloon—a signal to all concerned that it's still my turn. People are gathered around on the deck, spilling over into the grass. So many people. Everyone but Andre. *Where are Charles and his cousin?*

"We are so proud of Taja . . . of her accomplishments . . . of the young lady she's become," Mom continues. "And we know her future is bright . . . that her life is taking her to high places, where she will be successful . . . and blessed."

*High places* makes my ears leap, calling my mind to go away with it.

"Yes," Daddy joins in, "because we know God is always watching over her. Now if we can all join hands, I'd like to say a special prayer."

I steady the balloon between waist and elbow, stretch out both palms, bow my head, and let my mind go off to high places. Pine trees . . . a rooftop with a swing . . . a bridge to a place I've never been . . . a forty-story library, where I get lost, and the only words I catch of Daddy's prayer are *amen* and *glory be to God.*

"Let's eat cake!" Mom says, and clasps her hands in front of her chest.

In the center of the extra-large sheet cake, there's an image of the graduation photo I took at Olan Mills. Not the cap-and-gown one, the one of me sitting in a wingback chair in front of a library. Even though the library is fake, something about seeing myself sitting in front of so many books makes my head float.

Daddy puts his arm around my shoulders. "I'm so proud of you," he says, gives me a kiss on the cheek, and walks away.

"Naima, come help me cut the cake," Mom says.

Naima is standing in the grass behind the table with her friends. Right behind them, Cassie is standing with Keisha. Cassie waves at someone and I look and see Charles walking around the back corner of the house. But he's alone. *What happened to his cousin?* Cassie walks over to Charles and gives him a hello kiss. Then another boy comes around the corner. *That must be him.* He looks cute under the silver lights, but I'd need to be closer to give him *fwine* (can't just go around handing out *fwines*).

Naima steps up onto the deck and slaps at the balloon, but I turn away from her and she misses. "So! You're still out."

I ignore her and try to spy the cousin again, but he, Cassie, and Charles are gone. I crank my neck this way and that, looking through the crowd.

"Here, Taja," and Mom holds out a huge piece of cake,

my whole picture, with the books behind me and everything.

"What am I supposed to do with that?"

"Eat it," Mom says. "It will stay fresh in the fridge for a few days."

"'Cuz I'm so, so fresh," Damon says, and catches me off guard with a headlock.

"Hey," I protest, grab the balloon with both hands, and nudge him with my right elbow.

"Just because you're graduating doesn't change the fact that you're my little sis." He gently digs his knuckles into my scalp, says "Remember that," and lets go. "Ah, for me?" he sings, and reaches for the cake.

Mom turns away from him, shielding the cake with her body.

"Come on. I need some cake so I can get this party started again." His big black headphones are still around his neck, making him look official. Last year when he told me he'd started deejaying campus parties to get more girls, I rolled my eyes and didn't ask about it again. But he's actually pretty good.

"Well, this piece is for Taja," Mom says, still holding the cake away from Damon. "There's plenty more for everyone else. Here, Taja," and she extends my picture out to me.

"Thanks," and I situate the balloon between waist and

right elbow, place the cake on my left palm, and use my right hand to help keep it balanced.

"Why don't you just put that thing down," Mom suggests.

"I got it," I say, and when I turn back around, the cousin's thick, curvy lips and high-cheeked dimples and clear, dark skin are standing right in my face, even finer than Cassie promised.

"Congratulations," he says, staring into my eyes, like he's offering something precious.

My insides rush up to the center of my forehead to glimpse the treasure and my balloon bursts. Glitter flies everywhere—tiny flecks of gold catching light and shimmying through the air. Thin layers settle on our bodies and form a fine deposit on the cousin's face and hair, making us look like statues, frozen in time to capture our glory.

# Double Date

I want to say good-bye in the backseat of the car, end the evening side by side, behind Cassie and Charles, instead of face-to-face at my front door . . . give the cousin a one-armed hug with two pats on the back of his silky orange shirt. But vengeance tugs me one too many times. So I watch him open the door and step outside; and I scoot toward his scrawny figure and take his sweaty, outstretched palm.

In the street, the neighborhood girls are still playing double-Dutch. They've just finished the chorus and now it's the jumping girl's turn to rhyme:

*"My name is Robin; I'm number one.*

*My reputation is having fun.*

*So if you trippin', just back on up.*

*'Cuz this home girl don't take no stuff."*


*Hollywood now swingin'*, I sing along in my head before my date pulls me away. I know what he's trying to do as we walk toward my front door—his slim, limp fingers laced with mine, his moist fingertips drawing circles around my knuckles. But it's not working. So I help him out, imagine his fingers thicker, stronger, like Andre's—imagine his fingertips dryer, softer, like Andre's, and let the tingles roll in.

Standing on the welcome mat, he tells me I'm beautiful and strokes my lower jawbone from ear to chin with the backside of his hand—so corny, I want to laugh, but I let him think his game is working, disguise my amusement with a smile. He smiles, too, lips spread thin over his wide mouth. Then he leans in. I want to turn my face to the side, but vengeance tugs again, so I close my eyes.

I try to imagine kissing Andre's big bottom lip, but his lips aren't Andre's. They're too stiff. And his tongue is too wet, too soft, like a sandwich that's sat in the melting ice of a cooler too long. It keeps moving in the same fast circles, nothing like the slow, winding paths of Andre's gentle tongue.

And his breath doesn't help, smells like the hot dog he ate at the movies. I try breathing in as little as possible, but even the tiny whiffs make me sick.

Giggles from the street and I withdraw my mouth, back away until the air is clear. The cousin smiles like he's pleased with himself, but I can't smile, can't pretend to have enjoyed it. To be polite, I tell him I had a nice time. He believes me and asks for my number. I'm about to give him a fake one when I come up with a better idea, one that would kill two birds with one stone: give him Andre's.

# Sweet-Bitter
# Rounds

**W**eighing wrongs along a path in the park, we let tall pines turn into shadowy strangers, blacker than the night. Andre and I have never been on the trail so late, never been so far away from the lights of the playground where we usually stayed, competing to swing the highest: flinging our legs to the stars and talking mess in the air but sharing dreams on the earth between rounds.

On the dark path, Andre walks ahead, shouting wrongs at me over his shoulder. "I can't believe you kissed another dude," he says, and shoves a long branch out of his way that springs back and slings water in my face.

"You kissed LaToya first," I say, and walk around the branch, snatching a handful of wet leaves. "LaToya!" With each step, I try to focus on the cool, thick mud sliding over my sandals, between my toes, and the smell of the evening rain, still hanging heavy in the woods, that puffs up my nose—sweetness I need between wrongs.

"I can't believe you let another dude kiss you so easy," he says.

"*Easy?*" The word tastes salty in my mouth, making my top lip curl up and the skin above the bridge of my nose crouch down like it's ready for a fight. I want to lunge at the white Adidas sign on the back of his black T-shirt, make him fall chin first in the mud, but the word *easy* checks my steps, piercing my muscles and squeezing my bones. I think about throwing my handful of leaves at his head. Instead I scream, "You ignored all my calls, told everybody our business, and now you're telling me what you can't believe. Boy, please!" I tear one of the rubbery leaves down the center.

Andre walks farther away, yelling at me, but I'm tired of listening to him, so I let the song of the forest drown him out. I stand still, listening to the chirps, trills, cheeps, rustlings, flutters, and squeaks, tearing leaf after leaf until I only have twigs and a tiny, round thing left in my hand. I pick out the tiny ball and let the twigs fall to the ground.

Andre hurls a bunch of words over his right shoulder. He hurls them again. And again. Then he stops, twists his thick torso around toward the gap between us, and turns his long legs and feet to join the rest of his body. He approaches me, picking up where he left off: "You made me wait a whole month for a kiss, and then you go and kiss this dude on the first date. How could you be so easy?"

There's that word again—*easy*—catching hold of my insides, making me feel like some kind of warrior, fighting to defend them and break them free. "You kissed LaToya in my face!" An image of them kissing in front of the concession stand enters my mind and takes a front-row seat. I can feel myself about to cry, can feel the heat traveling up my chest to my face. I roll the tiny round ball between my first finger and thumb, trying to feel something else. The ball is firm and smooth, except for a single bump. I play with the bump—rolling the ball while trying to keep the bump inside the crease of my finger—but the heat still comes. I press the heat down from my eyes to my nose. Andre is only a few feet away—eyes cocky and cold, like he doesn't know me, like he thinks he's more than me. I refuse to let him see me cry, so I hold the tiny ball up to the stars. It's green . . . a newborn berry. I put it in my mouth and chew it—more bitter than Mom's morning grapefruit—but the heat cools.

"Everyone is talking about how easy you are. Some

people are even calling you a ho. Now I never called you a ho. My momma taught me better than to call a girl a ho. But everybody isn't brought up the same way. Some people call a ho a ho. They just can't help it." He stands over me looking happy with himself.

*No, he didn't just have the nerve to call me out of my name*, I think, and something lights up in the front part of my brain, something like a red arrow, pointing the way. My sadness quickly finds the exit. I want to be mad enough to slap him, like women do in movies, but my brain won't finger the impulse. All I can do is stare at his smirk and think about the ways he's hurt me, the word he's calling me, that nasty word—*ho*— more bitter than the green berry. I can't taste it, can't even defend myself against it. That word is numbing me, tearing a hole in me. He keeps talking and *ho* keeps running out of his mouth, into my ears, over my tongue, down my throat, through my chest, and exiting out of the bottom of my belly without catching taste bud, rib, or spleen. The old *easy*s are untying their ropes, reeling in their hooks, and escaping with the new *ho*s out of the hole. Sweet hole. I imagine licking its edge like a sugar-rimmed glass of lemonade. I run away with its sweetness, toward the light, to the swings.

When I get to the swings, I sit down in the wet rubber seat and allow my feet to sink deep in the puddle below—cool mud kissing my skinny ankles. I can see Andre running through the trees but when he gets to the playground, he quickly stops and strolls. I see right through his slow steps, see he still cares. But I don't. I've tried so hard not to care after all the times he hurt me, but there were always parts of him still curled up in my corners. I'm almost happy he called me a ho, yes, happy he delivered the last blow that tore me open.

I grab the metal chains, push my toes against the wet earth, and lean back, kick forward, lean back, and kick forward until I'm swinging in a world of tiny lights. Up and over to the right, a bright one flickers, maybe a newborn star. I kick my feet stronger and lean back farther to go higher and higher—reaching. With the warm wind rolling over my shoulders and mud drying on my ankles and toes, my insides feel free. I watch my muddy pinky toe touch the blinking star, and taste what seems to be a million sprinkles of sweetness on my tongue—tiny balls of promise. I picture myself at Stanford, making friends with strangers and taking notes on the first pages of my fresh notebooks—my name written in their top right-hand corners. Taja Brown.

As God's strong arm brings me closer to the ground, I look down and notice Andre—belly draped over the other swing, stretched out, drawing circles in the mud with a stick. I guess he feels my gaze because he turns his head my way, drops his stick, and stands up. "I'm sorry," he says, stepping behind me, grabbing the rubber seat around my hips. After he brings me to a stop, he says, "I'm sorry," again, lets go of the seat, and walks around to face me.

Somehow his face looks different, ugly—an ugliness his apologies can never erase. I imagine his remorseful words passing right through me into the night air, still scented with rain and pine, then drifting off and getting lost somewhere in the woods.

"I'm sorry for everything. I was stupid," he says. I look at the watery whites of his eyes, at the bright bodies in the sky beyond them, and then at my watch, which reads ten twenty-six. "Can't we just press rewind . . . forget," he says, his words starting to crack. He lowers his knees into the mud, his heavy head in my lap. I let him because I know he can taste my indifference, know it's not sweet to him like it is to me. But I start to feel the heat of his face on my inner thighs through my jeans. *No.* I can't allow myself to feel him cry. *Oh, no.* I can't allow his tears to seep through my pores and find the places that can love him. So I stand up and walk off, leaving him on his knees in the mud.

On the way home, I ride with my window down, breeze rolling over my cheeks, staring at the bright balls in the sky and the invisible lines in between, knowing it will be my last ride in the Cutlass Supreme.

# Forget That

*S*in is winning with six. I'm keeping score on my church bulletin. Including all versions of the word—sin, sinner, sinned, sinning, and sinful—*sin* always leads the words most spoken during church. *Hallelujah* is never too far behind because I count the one the congregation passes around: up, up it goes, giving glory to God, and slowly falls back down. Then like a beach ball at a graduation ceremony—Hallelujah!—someone else sends it back up without letting it touch the ground.

The announcements are slow, most words resting in neutral, taking a break from the race. At the podium, Sister

Davis reads them through her hot pink lips, shifting her weight between baby-oiled legs after each sentence. "Next Sunday there will be a bake sale after church in the fellowship hall." She rocks one hip up, sleek calf sliding past sleek calf, kissing beneath her pencil skirt. One hip down, red high heels holding their ground. "All proceeds will go toward scholarships for Vacation Bible School." I'm back in business: a point for *church*, *fellowship*, and *Bible*. That's five for *Bible*; *Bible* gets a cross slash. "That's all the announcements I have for you this morning. God bless." She turns away from the microphone, clears her throat, and turns back, "Yes, God bless us all." That's four for *bless* and six, no, seven for *God*.

"What's wrong with her?" Keisha whispers in my ear.

I lie with a shrug. Sister Davis doesn't need anybody else in her business. I didn't need to be in her business, but I couldn't help putting my ear to the closed door after I saw Pastor Hayes take her by the elbow and lead her into his office before Bible study last Wednesday. Pastor Hayes surely didn't need to be in her business, but that didn't stop him from telling her she needed to dress more appropriately if she wanted to continue reading the announcements every Sunday, suggesting looser skirts, lighter lipstick, and panty hose.

As Sister Davis walks away from the podium, down the

red-carpeted aisle, Deacon Boyd stands up in the front row. He's a short man, standing only a head taller than my daddy sitting down—thank God it's not my daddy's turn to pray; we'd be here all day. Deacon Boyd walks to the podium, pulls down the microphone, and says, "Please rise." That's three for *rise*, and I slide my bulletin inside my Bible before I stand up and reach across the aisle for Sister Price's hand, my left palm up so she knows to put her hand in mine. My hands don't like to be held. They start to tingle, go dead. Keisha already knows this and gives me her hand, but my left palm is still empty. So I turn toward Sister Price and see Sister Davis in the aisle, trapped behind the hooked hands of the row ahead, holding her clutch purse under her arm, her Bible to her chest.

"Excuse me," Sister Davis says. The hands release and she squeezes through.

I lower my arm, step out of the aisle to widen the path, and Sister Davis walks past the last row, smelling lilac sweet. As the trail of purple flowers shrinks, Sister Price extends her hand, and I step back into the aisle, close the gap.

"Let us pray," Deacon Boyd says. Another point for *pray* and the congregation bows its head, but I turn back to look at the double doors, swinging.

*Focus, Taja.* This is the hard part: keeping track of words while my hands are tied up in prayer. Good thing Deacon

Boyd's prayers are as short as his legs. Add one to *heaven*. One to *Father*. *Pray* again. Okay, that's *pray, heaven, Father, pray*. One more for *bless*. That's *pray, heaven, Father, pray, bless*. One more for *forgive*. Another for *sin*. That's *pray, heaven, Father, pray, bless, forgive, sin. Sin* again. And again. That's *pray, heaven, Father, pray, bless, forgive, sin, sin, sin*. One more for *save*. Add *deliver*. Add *heal*. Add *sickness*. That's *pray, heaven, Father, pray, bless, forgive, sin, sin, sin, save, deliver, heal, sickness*. "Hallelujah!" says someone sitting behind me. "Hallelujah!" shouts someone across the aisle. One more for *Jesus*. Another for *mercy*. "Hallelujah!" again and again. One more for *pray*. *Amen*. That's *pray, heaven, Father, pray, bless, forgive, sin, sin, sin, save, deliver, heal, sickness, hallelujah, hallelujah, Jesus, mercy, hallelujah, hallelujah, pray, amen*. I release the hands in my hands, sit down, and make my marks with a blue felt-tip pen.

"Hallelujah," I hear again, but I can't count it because the choir is singing, and I don't tally during songs, too sacred. That would be wrong. Voices swoop, soar as the choir sways from side to side, clapping their hands in red robes with sleeves like wings. I clap my hands, too, my right elbow tapping Keisha's left arm on the off beats. Sister Wallace stands up in front of us, her wide butt jiggling in our face, laughing at us under her maroon dress. Forget that. We stand up, sing along, and two-step—fun except Keisha is off beat, and it's hard to keep my rhythm beside confused hands and feet.

On the other side of Keisha, Mona and Brandy whip forward, laughing in their seats, and almost hit their big foreheads on the wooden pew. Dang! That would have been good. Today Keisha thinks she's jamming: bobbing her head and rocking her hips. Her mind doesn't have a clue that her body is as in sync with the music as English words are with Bruce Lee's lips. I think about leaning over and whispering the truth in her ear, the truth that taps me on the shoulder every Sunday and says, *A friend would tell*. Yes, a friend would tell the truth so no one could ever laugh at her again. No, forget that. Telling the truth would be a sin. And I'd be a sinner every Sunday if I made Keisha think twice about standing up and clapping her hands. So what if she dances like a white girl. At least she likes moving to the rhythm God put in her ear.

The next song is slow and we sit down. The notes rise higher than hallelujah in the sky and return like sprinkles, soft beats that tingle. I let them sink in.

"Give another round of applause for this magnificent choir," Pastor Hayes says, walking into the pulpit, clapping his hands, black sleeves flapping. Time to start tallying again. "God is good!" he yells into the microphone.

"All the time!" the congregation answers.

"All the time!" he continues.

"God is good!"

That's five for *good* and seven for *God*. Pastor Hayes begins every sermon the same way, so *God* always picks up a few points, needed points, too, since people in church like to replace *God* with *Lord, Jesus, Savior, Holy Spirit,* and *Heavenly Father*. Wait. Did Pastor Hayes just say *Bible*? He sure did because I hear thin pages turning—*swish, swish, swish*—to find the scripture. That's three for *Bible*. Let me pay attention.

Four for *evil*. Add *wrong*, that's one. *Die*: two. Eleven for *Lord*. Add *desire*. Add *heart*. Another one for *Lord*. *Trust*: one. "Hallelujah!" That's fourteen. One more for *Lord*. And another. *Trust*: two. Five for *righteous*. *Wait*: eight. *Patiently*: seven. Add *justice*. Three for *wicked*. "Hallelujah!" Add *anger*. Add *wrath*. Five for *evil*. No, six for *evil*. One more for *Lord*. One more for *wicked*. *Found*: one. Add *meek*. Add *peace*. Five for *wicked*. *Righteous*: six. Fifteen for *Lord*. Add *laugh*. Six for *wicked*. *Coming*: one.

*Lord* came up in the scripture reading, only one away from *sin*. But *sin* is just warming up. Did a few lunges during the prayers. A few stretches, high knees, and laps around the track. But during Pastor Hayes's bullet points, *sin* is about to all-out sprint. *Sin*: seventeen. I wasn't playing. *Die*: three. Add *lie*. *Die*: four. Add *believers*. Seven for *mercy*. Eight for *save*.

"Hallelujah!" That's sixteen. Add *punish*. *Sin*: eighteen. *Sin*: nineteen. Add *surrender*. Three for *temptation*. Add *earth*. One more for *wait*. Nine for *heaven*. "Hallelujah!" Four for *deliver*. *Blood*: ten. *Jesus*: thirteen. "Hallelujah!" *Born* again. One, no, two more for *sin*.

Tallying keeps me busy so I don't have to listen—add *eternity*, *hell*—and makes me look like I'm paying attention. *Heaven*: ten. *Save*: nine. *Soul*: three. Pretty clever if I may say so myself, but it's not for everybody. Fourteen for *Jesus*. "Hallelujah!" That's seventeen. Keisha tried it a few times— another point for *God*—but it was too much work, so now she's back to writing Pastor Hayes's bullet points inside the lined box with "Sermon Notes" printed at the top. *Son*: three. *Sin*: twenty. She's on the last line of her second bullet point: "Don't be jealous of sinners who flaunt their sins because they will spend eternity in hell while you're in heaven."

"Hallelujah!" That's eighteen. Forget bullet points and writing sermon notes on lines in a box. *Patiently*: eight. The first thing I do every Sunday is write, "Church Words" over "Sermon Notes" with thick blue ink. Add *brothers*. Add *sisters*. Eleven for *heaven*. "Hallelujah!" And there's no telling where the box or lines are anymore on my bulletin—wait, *hallelujah* is only one away from *sin*. *Jesus*: fifteen. "Hallelujah!" *Save*: ten. "Hallelujah!" *Hallelujah* just took the lead! I look down at Keisha's sermon notes. She's on the last line of her third bullet point. *Hallelujah* could win. *Jesus* again. And again. When Pastor Hayes starts screaming "Jesus" that means the end is near. Another blue mark for *Jesus*—that's nineteen—even *Jesus* could win!

Pastor Hayes paces the stage while wiping his sweat and breathing heavily into the microphone. After he preaches, he always does this for a few minutes to add drama or maybe to catch his breath from all the screaming, probably both. The whole choir is looking straight at the director playing the organ, waiting for their cue. Come on, choir. When the choir starts singing, the race is over because they don't stop until the closing prayer, which is always the same: *Lord keep us until we meet again.* And while that's an extra point for *Lord*, *Lord* only has—let me see—three blue fences, that's fifteen points, not enough to win.

My bulletin is covered with short lines and cross slashes—blue picket fences traveling off the page, tallying the church's words, little blue reminders that the words are not God's. I don't even know if God has words unless I count the high-pitched sound I hear when I get still, but that's not really a word. It's more like a one-note song always on repeat. The director starts playing the organ. If I had to give God's one-note song a word, then I would pick *hallelujah* or *love*.

Yes, Jesus would love *love*! But *love* wasn't spoken today. The director waves his hand and the choir stands. "Are you saved?" Pastor Hayes says, panting into the microphone. Uh-oh, here he goes again. That's one more for *saved*. "When you lay your head down at night, do you know where you will go if you die before you wake? Do you?" *Die*: five. The director waves his hand again, and the choir starts to sing. Yes! *Hallelujah* wins! "Do you want Jesus to forgive you of your sins? If you do, then come." The choir is singing so I can't count anymore. But Pastor Hayes holds up his right hand, a signal for the choir to stop singing, and the choir follows his command. He repeats, "Do you want Jesus to forgive you for your sins?" No, forget that. *Hallelujah* already won. I'm done.

# Calling
# My Name

In the hush of an early Sunday morning, I hear a call, a one-note song floating across my dreaming skies    a sweet cue for me to open my eyes. Outside my window, the world is a pool of softness: hues of purple, blue, and rose, delicacy I want to dive into.

Without wiping sleep from the corners of eyes or brushing teeth, and before alarms can go off, phones ring, toilets flush, or voices find themselves, I step outside.

In only pajamas, I walk out to edge of the front lawn, dew wetting my feet. How amazingly still, how sacred the street seems in the light of early morning: no one mowing lawns, riding bikes, honking, screaming, laughing, dribbling, kicking, crying, or playing hide-and-seek. It's like an empty sanctuary, only me inside, front row, heart tolling like the ten-o'clock worship bell.

Something buzzes into existence near my right ear. I turn, look, and it's gone. A green and violet swallow, perched on our mailbox, stretches open its beak as if taking its first breath of morning and speaks to me in a high-pitched tongue—a call for birds, unseen in the low bushes along the house and in the high balconies of the cedar elm tree in the center of our yard, to do the same. I stand swaying to the hymn of what seems like hundreds of chirps rippling through the air.

In the sky overhead, the last hints of purple and pink dissolve into blue, which gets lighter by the second as a soft-gold arch reaches higher above the row of sloped roofs.

A whistling wind blows through, first pressing against my lips, then digging into my left ear, next rubbing the nape of my neck and the backs of my bare legs. I watch the invisible hand move along the street through the trees, tops following the wind's direction, but trunks, rooted to the land that bore them, standing still.

Something is crawling on my left foot. I look down, see a red ant, and reach down to slap it off. As I bend over, the gold cross, hanging from my neck, swings and taps my forehead—my going-away gift from last night reminding me of its presence.

"It holds all of our love and prayers," Daddy said, after dinner, before ice cream and cobbler, and clasped the chain around my neck, rough fingers brushing my spine.

"And eyes and ears," Damon said, smiling, home for the weekend, sporting a new goatee. "So don't think just because you'll be halfway across the country, you can get away with anything."

"You can sleep and shower in it, and it won't turn green," Naima said.

"She's right, it's pure. Won't ever tarnish or fade," Mom added.

I touch the gold cross, warm on my chest, feel another ant crawl over the edge of my right foot, and think about running out of the grass to the driveway. But something about the warmth won't let me.

After a few moments, I feel the wind behind me again, pressing the backs of my knees. I walk with it to a place bare of grass beneath our tree. A few loose leaves rain down and stroke the skin of my right shoulder and cheek. I look up and see patches of bright light peeking through shivering green. Bits of sun spill down on me, cling to me, and I fling my arms wide open and spin round and round with the wind on all sides of me, lifting my hair off my shoulders, my feet up to their toes, directing the movements of my very first Sunday solo.

Around me, the wind slows, but inside me it whirls on, faster and faster until I can't keep myself up over the center of my soles, so I sit down and lean back against the tree. Two of its large roots rest just outside each of my outstretched legs, like the way Mom used to sit behind me when she braided my hair.

Next door, the dog barks, as if to warn me that the rest of the world will soon be up, and I imagine the mystery of my morning curling up and fading like smoke.

Then something hums fiercely in my right ear, but before I turn, it disappears. With my eyes, I follow the buzz to the row of firebushes along the front of the house, where I see a hummingbird, first hovering, tail flapping up and down, wings beating too fast to see, then darting from fiery flute to fiery flute in search of something sweet.

Its long, skinny beak must have found all the nectar it needs because it speeds off, crossing my face so close, I feel the breeze of its wings against my cheeks.

Heart tinkling, I lean my head back against the tree, closing my eyes. Beams of light stream down through the leaves and warm the mole in middle of my forehead, the one on the tip of my nose, and my favorite one in the triangle above my left collarbone. A light seems to vibrate on the thick of my earlobes, whispering something personal to me. My insides climb a thousand scales to get closer, to listen to the light. Up, up, I rise. I'm a gospel song in my highest, purest note, in perfect harmony with what calls to me.

"Taja."

I've never heard my name sound so infinitely clear, as if stretched out forever, over millions of miles and years.

"Taja."

I melt into it and feel it flow into me and out of me like waves.

"Taja!"

Something shifts in a faraway place, and I open my eyes and see Mom standing over me in her white robe.

"What in the world are you doing out here in your pajamas?" she says, tightening the robe's belt around her waist.

I'm about to tell her when I stop, afraid of her response.

"Have you gone deaf? I asked you a question. Don't think just because you're about to leave for college you can start ignoring me."

No excuses come to me. There's only the truth, flickering inside me like the patches of light shifting on Mom's angry face. The truth, making me feel like I can trust it, its beauty, its goodness, its grace, like I could rest the weight of my whole being upon it. "Having church," I say.

"Church? No, church is what you're about to get your butt up and get ready for," she says, and extends her hand.

But I know by the way she looks at me, curiously then reverentially, by the way she blinks twice without pause, and by the high rise in her tone, that she understands me, so I smile and I take her hand.

As my weight comes back over my soles, I feel my right foot itch and reach down to scratch a small, red bite. Then Mom says, "Look!" I turn and see a butterfly whipping its white-tipped wings over my left shoulder, then in front of me, above me, beyond the roof of the house, and gone.